SPIN
TRUTH, TUBAS AND GEORGE WASHINGTON

DAVE AND NETA JACKSON

STORY AND CHARACTERS BASED ON THE
MINI-MOVIE™ OF THE SAME
NAME WRITTEN AND CREATED BY GEORGE TAWEEL & ROB LOOS

BROADMAN
& HOLMAN
PUBLISHERS

Nashville, Tennessee

Copyright © 1994

BROADMAN & HOLMAN PUBLISHERS

TAWEEL-LOOS & COMPANY
"The mini-movie™ Studio"

"SPIN" is based on the Story and Teleplay written by
George Taweel & Rob Loos. © 1993.

4240-04
0-8054-4004-6

Dewey Decimal Classification: JF
Subject Heading: HONESTY - FICTION
Library of Congress Card Catalog Number: 93-50903
Printed in the United States of America

Library of Congress Cataloging-in-Publication Data
Jackson, Dave.
    Spin : truth, tubas, and George Washington / by Dave and Neta
Jackson.
        p. cm. — (Secret adventures)
    "Based on the video of the same name created by George
Taweel & Rob Loos."
    Summary: Drea Thomas, running against her nemesis Arlene
for president of her seventh grade class, fears that she is falling
into the same dishonest campaign tactics she despises in her
opponent.
    ISBN 0-8054-4004-6
    [1. Politics, Practical—Fiction.   2. Schools—Fiction.
3. Honesty—Fiction.]   I. Jackson, Neta.   II. Taweel, George.
III. Loos, Rob.   IV. Title.   V. Series: Jackson, Dave. Secret
adventures.
PZ7.J132418Sk 1994
[Fic]—dc20   93-50903
                                                            CIP

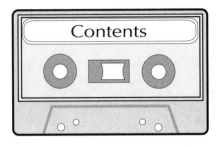

Contents

Truth stands the test of time; lies are soon exposed.

—Proverbs 12:19, TLB

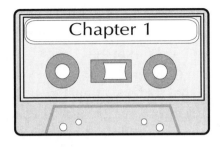

Cutting Grass and Pangosass

Testing . . . testing. Is this thing working? *Dad!* How do I get this Walkman to record? . . . It is? Okay, okay, I'll play it back and see if I'm getting anything. Wait a minute . . . Which button is supposed to stop this thing?

— *Click!* —

All right! That wasn't so hard. Guess I won't flunk Push-Buttons 101 after all. Now let's see . . . *Dad!* This is a private conversation between me and my Walkman! Know what I mean? Why don't you go win a Grammy or something . . . *please?*

— *Click!* —

Hmmm, probably shouldn't be so hard on Dad. After all, he did get me this Walkman as a graduation present from sixth grade. But I've got plans for you, Sir Walkman . . . *Sir* Walkman? *Not!* Hmmm . . . Willie Walkman? . . . Wanda Walkwoman? . . . That's pretty lame, Drea Thomas.

You see, electronic-whatever-you-are, I've tried to write in those cute little diaries that Aunt Beth sends me every Christmas, but all I do is feel guilty at all the blank pages. I'm not sure how to tell her that a hot pink "Girl-Talk One Year Diary" isn't exactly my style. For one thing, it would take too long to actually write down all the outrageous things that go spinning in my head on any given day.

So . . . when Dad gave me this Walkman, I got this great idea! Why not an *electronic diary*—you know, like, *ahem!* "Star Date, Two Thousand and Ten. Captain Kirk here." Then I could . . .

Wait. That's it! That's it! Absolute-o perfect-o! It's so obvious I couldn't see it with my eyes crossed.

Ahem. Drum roll, Maestro!

I, Drea Thomas, owner of what was once a simple tape recorder, do dub thee "Electronic Diary," or "E.D." for short. From now on, E.D., it's for better or worse, for richer or poorer, in sickness or in health, till death or electronic failure do us part—and *everything* that passes between us is strictly SECRET!

And, if my dad or even my best friend Kimb
Andow ever tries to listen to this tape—SHUT THIS
THING OFF RIGHT NOW, YOU SNOOPS!

Guess I gotta go, E.D.—I hear Grandpa calling
me. He promised to show me how to start the power
lawn mower once Dad left for his office at the college. I mean, I'm going into seventh grade, and it
feels pretty stupid to have Timmy Krakowski, who's
only going into sixth, earning five bucks a week to
mow our lawn. If Drea Thomas can't mow a lawn
and be earning that five bucks, I ought to have my
head examined!

— Click! —

Back again, E.D. Maybe this lawn mowing
thing is overrated. Is there some rule in New
Jersey that says all lawn mowers have to be thirty
years old? And with all the humidity, the grass
clippings stick to everything . . . and I mean everything! Grass in my ears, grass in my hair, grass in
my socks . . .

At least I hope Dad pays me. It's not like I asked
him or anything, but the deal makes sense to me,
right? I wanted to prove to him I could do it. And
the cutting part was easy . . . once I got the machine
going. Why is it so hard pulling that rip cord, anyway? Grandpa kept saying, "Easy, easy," as I was
pulled by the rewind back toward the motor! Man,
you need to be a weight lifter to get one of those

things started . . . Hey! Maybe I've started a new exercise craze: MOWERCIZE! "Trim your grass and lose weight at the same time!"

Anyway. Sweat was really pouring down my back by the time I finished both the front *and* the back yards. Grandpa was still weeding in his vegetable garden—okay, he calls it "his" because he's the only one in the family who gardens—and I saw him wiping his face with his big red bandana—there's nothing like New Jersey humidity in the middle of summer to work up a thirst. So I figured we could both use some iced tea. I really put together a wild brew this time, E.D., and Grandpa . . .

Oh. I really should introduce my family if I'm going to start an electronic diary—for posterity, ya know.

Grandpa Ben is my dad's dad. He's been a railroad man all his life, but he hung up his conductor's hat last year. I was kinda worried that he'd go nuts giving up his familiar "All aboooooard!"—especially since Grandma died several years ago—but after he retired he decided our garden had been neglected long enough. He's over here practically every day zapping weeds or pruning the tomatoes to perfection.

Mom wanted Grandpa Ben to move in with us—guess she was afraid he was getting too old to live by himself. After all, there's only the three of us—Mom, Dad, and me—in this big house so we'd

have plenty of room. But Grandpa wouldn't hear of it. Said he's been independent and set in his ways too long to play second fiddle in a family as crazy and busy as ours. But . . . Grandpa's over here a lot anyway and I like it. It's kinda like having a big brother around—well, not really, 'cause he doesn't listen in on my phone calls or steal my CD's like my friends' big brothers do—but he's always willing to sit and listen to me, and he tells me stuff, you know, gives me things to think about.

Like today.

I came out of the house with a pitcher of my ice-cold special brew and two glasses. Grandpa Ben saw me coming and smiled—he's got the greatest laugh wrinkles all around his eyes. They make his eyes twinkle.

"I hope that's for me," he said, wiping his forehead with the bandana one more time.

"Yep," I said, "brewed it myself. Special 'Grandpa flavored' iced tea."

I poured him a glass and Grandpa took a long drink.

"Like it?" I asked.

He made polite Grandpa noises, like, "Ummmm-hmmmmm." But I wasn't going to let him get off so easy. I mean, this was a great concoction, never before tasted on the face of this planet, much less in Hampton Falls, New Jersey.

"Honestly?" I asked, and gave him my you-better-tell-me-the truth look.

"Sure!" he said, and this time I believed him. So I poured myself a big glass and decided to divulge my secret. "I call it 'Pangosass'—passion fruit, mango, and sassafras tea all mixed together."

Grandpa's eyebrows went up and he looked kinda funny at the tea he held in his hand. But, good sport that he is, he took another drink.

"Still like it?" I asked. I knew I was pushing, but it's not every day I come up with a special blend that works—I mean, some of them have to be thrown out, although Mom's always telling me, "If you make it, you eat it" . . . or drink it, depending on what the concoction is.

But Grandpa was sold. "Uh-huh. Tastes even better this time," he said. "As your great-grandpa always used to say—"

Now that's something you gotta get used to about my grandpa, E.D. Great-grandfather Thomas was a preacher, and Grandpa's always quoting stuff his father used to tell him. But this time I was ready for him, and I jumped in before he could finish.

"'Truth stands the test of time, lies are soon exposed,'" I finished for him. That's somewhere in Proverbs I think.

Grandpa laughed. "Have I said that before?"

"Once or twice or a dozen times," I told him, but he knew I was teasing. Grandpa went back to pulling weeds from around his tomato plants, and it made me wonder: "Did great-grandpa like to garden, too?"

"Oh, sure," Grandpa nodded. "He filled his sermons with talk about gardening. He always told me, 'If you can understand what makes things grow, you're well on the way to understanding life.'"

I just sat and watched Grandpa work for a while. Maybe that's why Grandpa is so smart about life—he's good at growing vegetables and flowers. But I don't think lawns count as "gardening." When I finished cutting the grass, I didn't feel any smarter—only tireder.

Finally, he held out his glass and asked for "another glass of that iced tea."

See what I'm up against, E.D.? Grandpa's great, but he still doesn't realize that you can't call a Drea Special by an ordinary name like "iced tea."

"*Pangosass*," I corrected him, but I poured him another glass anyway.

Grandpa drank the whole thing. "Whatever ya call it, it's swell, Drea."

"Truth?" I asked—but this time I knew the answer.

"Truth," he said.

See what I mean, E.D.? I'm not exactly sure what Grandpa means when he says, "Truth stands the test of time, but lies are soon exposed" . . . but it's something to think about.

Well, better sign off. Tomorrow is orientation day for the new seventh graders at Hampton Falls Junior High. Can't wait! This year is going to be so cool. But I'm a little nervous, too . . . I heard junior high is a lot tougher and everybody gets all weird—adolescence, ya know. But . . . I'm already weird, so I guess I'll be fine!

G'night, E.D.

— Click! —

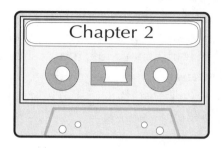

Battle of the Baby-sitters

G'morning, E.D.! Welcome to my third floor hideaway, up under the eaves along with the cobwebs and pigeons.

Just kidding about the pigeons.

Actually, the room my dad fixed for me from half of the attic is really great. My parents let me decorate it myself. Frankly, a slanted ceiling has certain advantages. I can actually look at my maps and posters while lying in bed without getting a crick in my neck. As for the rest, I'd call my decorating style, . . . um, "Early Attic."

Anyway. According to my mighty morphing watch—which looks to ordinary mortals like any other teen watch with a neon-colored strap and glow-in-the-dark numbers—it's Day 4,825 in the Secret Adventures of Drea Thomas. Isn't that a totally awesome thought? I figured it out: I have lived on this earth four thousand, eight hundred, and twenty-five days . . . hmmm. Wonder what that works out to in minutes? Or *seconds*?

Unfortunately, that's a humongous slice of my life—thirteen years!—already gone by unrecorded . . . *not* good for posterity. But I probably wasn't very articulate at age two, so I guess junior high is as good a place as any to start my electronic diary.

Good news! Dad gave me five dollars for doing the lawn and said I could have the job through September. Which means I'm going to have to think of some other way to earn money the rest of the school year.

Now, I know it's only orientation day, and school doesn't start for another week. But first impressions count! So . . . what should I wear that's really *me*? Overalls, baggy shirt, and saddle shoes? Plaid blazer, striped shirt, and jeans? Short tie? Long tie? Melon-colored hat? Aiiiieeeee! Too many decisions!

Oh—hang on. There's the phone.

Drea's Attic . . . oh, hi, Kimberly . . . twenty minutes?! I haven't even decided what to wear! . . . okay, okay, thirty minutes. I mean, we don't wanna look *too* eager . . . what? . . . Of course I want to see George Easton—he's a good friend of mine. . . .

Now just a minute, Kimberly Andow. I said *just* a friend, got it? . . . Okay, okay. 'Bye.

Now, where did I throw that blazer? . . . Uh-oh. I left the Walkman on . . .

— *Click!* —

Unbelievable, E.D. You will never guess what happened at orientation!

We had just finished the welcome-to-your-new-school pep-talk by Mrs. Long, the principal—she's great, by the way—when Kimberly and I saw a notice on the bulletin board by the office. It said:

NEEDED: Regular after-school baby-sitter, three afternoons a week, starting September. Two children, ages 6 and 9.

And it was signed by the principal!

See? It's perfect! If I can get a regular baby-sitting job, I'll be all set for spending money. Mom and Dad have made it pretty clear they're not about to increase my allowance. As long as they're doling out the money, however, they also have veto power on how I use it. But with my own job, I'll have enough to take advantage of clothes sales when they come along, and maybe even start saving for something like . . . like sky-diving lessons!

Kimberly, however, wasn't impressed. "You've *got* to be kidding," she said, rolling those big dark eyes at me. "Baby-sitting for the *principal*? Get real, Drea. If something goes wrong, you'll have permanent detention for the rest of the year!"

Oh, I forgot. I haven't introduced you to Kimberly yet, E.D. She's been my best and dearest friend since kindergarten. Her name is Kimberly Andow, she wants to be an actress, and if good looks count, she's gonna knock 'em dead. She's got dreamy skin to die for, set off by long dark hair. That's because her mother is French and her father is Japanese—isn't that exotic? My father thinks she's a little weird and wishes I had more friends to "balance out Kimberly"—whatever that means—but one thing for sure: there's never a boring moment with Kimberly around.

Anyway, back to the baby-sitting notice.

"Pessimist," I accused her. "Mrs. Long wouldn't give her baby-sitter detention . . . I don't think."

"Pessimist, no; realist, yes," Kimberly said breathily, doing her best Darryl Hannah imitation. Then she poked me. "Chill out, Drea. Here comes competition."

I looked around and saw Arlene Blake coming regally down the hall like some golden-haired goddess, wearing a matching "outfit" from Gucci's or someplace—I guess she likes that kind of stuff. Arlene is probably the most popular girl in our class—if by popular you mean being able to turn the heads of 99 percent of the boys in school. (The other one percent are either blind or dead.) Which, of course, doesn't always make her popular with the *girls*—except those who hope to gain prestige by hovering in Arlene's shadow . . . like Marcy Mannington.

Poor Marcy. She could be pretty, with that great naturally curly hair, if she'd give up those mousy dresses. But I think Arlene doesn't want anyone close to her who might outshine her.

Today, as usual, Marcy was *trying* to walk beside Arlene, but was being edged out by one of Arlene's panting admirers—a short guy, new I think. When Arlene saw us, she stopped suddenly, causing the poor dude to bump his nose on her shoulder blade. Kimberly snorted and poked me again. But I didn't laugh; I felt sorry for him— especially when Arlene gave him an icy stare. Then she turned on her smile for us—you know, the kind that is sticky sweet.

"Are you thinking about baby-sitting the Long children, Andrea?" she asked me.

That was her first mistake, E.D. Nobody, but *nobody*, calls me Andrea . . . except my parents when they're mad at me. I could feel my blood beginning to boil.

"I hope you won't be too disappointed, Andrea," she went on. "I already gave Mrs. Long one of my business cards, and she said she was going to call me this afternoon as soon as orientation is over."

Our mouths dropped open. *Business cards?* It was all Kimberly and I could do to keep from rolling on the floor right there.

Then—get this, E.D.—Arlene *tossed* her hair, like some TV commercial for hair shampoo, and sailed down the hall with the same short guy following in her wake, rubbing his nose.

Can you believe it, E.D.? Baby-sitting business cards!

Well, business cards or not, I'm going to call Mrs. Long about that baby-sitting job. Two can play this game.

Over and out. Wish me luck, E.D.

— Click! —

Oh, forgot to say I saw George Easton at orientation today. He's lookin' *good* with that summer tan. Glad we can be friends—and I hope it stays that way. 'Cause every girl in seventh grade is gonna have a crush on him.

— Click! —

One more thing, E.D. Today the principal said that the eighth grade had elected its class officers last spring. But since the seventh graders are new to the junior high, we would have our election the third week of September.

Kimberly and George ganged up on me after orientation and told me I ought to run for class president. I appreciate their confidence, but I'm not very interested in politics. I'd like to get used to junior high first and make sure I can handle the homework before jumping into stuff. Besides, I want to try out for soccer.

— Click! —

Bad news, E.D. I called the principal, Mrs. Long, tonight. She said Arlene Blake had already applied for the job and was going to baby-sit for her this weekend as a trial run. Then she said, "But if something else comes up before I have to make my decision, I'll be sure to call you."

Yeah, right. As if I'll have a chance once Arlene turns on the charm. I might as well forget it. Who can compete with her stupid business cards? She probably does it "by the book"—ya know, *Arlene Blake's Guide to Perfect Baby-sitting.*

Trouble is, that job would have been so perfect! Now what am I gonna do—shovel snow?

— Click! —

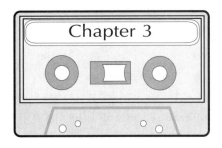

Baby-sitting Blues

Guess what, E.D.? A few minutes ago . . . oh, wait. Better date this for posterity. It's been six days since my last entry, which makes it, uh . . . Day 4,831 in the Secret Adventures of Drea Thomas. The place is the kitchen. The time: fifteen hundred hours—that's three P.M. to normal humans.

Anyway. A few minutes ago I answered the phone and guess who it was? Mrs. Long! She said something else *had* come up—a reception or something for new teachers this coming Friday—and she asked if I wanted to baby-sit for Rebecca and Matt. Those are her kids . . . Rebecca is nine and Matt is six. Anyway, I said yes, even though Friday *is* the last day of summer vacation—not counting Labor

23

Day weekend. Still, it's worth it for a chance to get that baby-sitting job.

But I gotta think of something to do with the kids that'll be fun . . . Hey! Are those fresh blueberries sitting on the kitchen counter? I wonder if Grandpa picked 'em and brought us some. Mmmm, I love blueberries . . . guess I'll get out the colander and wash some and . . .

Whoa! Where do you critters think you're hightailing it to? Come back here, you little blue bandits! No . . . no! Not into the dish water! Who wants soap suds with their blueberries? Come back here . . . aha! Got one, two . . . three . . . uh, oh! There go some over the edge . . . onto the floor . . . under the refrigerator!

All right, Drea Thomas, you oughta be a match for a gang of blueberries. Cut 'em off at the pass! Scoop 'em into the colander . . . zap 'em with the sink sprayer . . . there. That's better. Now I'll just get a few paper towels—

Hey! Cut it out, you guys. Give me back those towels! Oh, all right. Go ahead and do a shimmy in the shower . . . just—don't—sing! And no snapping those towels, either, even if they are only paper!

Sorry, E.D. My imagination got a little carried away washing those blueberries. But it gave me an idea of what to do with the Long kids . . . blueberry muffins! All kids like to eat. If I took some blueberries Friday, I could make muffins with Rebecca and what's-his-name, her little brother—oh, yeah, Matt.

Over and out. Gotta call Kimberly and tell her the news. Or maybe I'll tell Grandpa Ben first. Gotta ask if I can use some of his blueberries, anyway.

— *Click!* —

Later, same day.

You'll never guess what my dad came home with tonight, E.D.—a sousaphone! That monster is so big he could hardly get it in the house! And to think that he considers Kimberly and me weird! Why can't he stick with a nice violin, or a jazz saxaphone? But being a music professor at Hampton Falls Junior College sure gives him some strange ideas. Now he wants to write a "Sonata for Sousaphone" . . . give me a break. I may never survive my parents, much less junior high! At least Grandpa's

got his feet planted on the ground. (Sorry, Grandpa—bad pun.)

Over and out.

— *Click!* —

Day 4,834 in the Secret Adventures of Drea Thomas. I'm on my way to the Long house right now, E.D., on my trusty Western Flyer . . .

For the sake of any great-grandchildren listening to these memoirs who will wonder why Great-Grandmother Drea was riding a Western Flyer in the 1990s, the age of mountain bikes and zillion-speed racers . . . that's exactly the point. Everyone and their trained lizard has a mountain bike or racing bike. But no one has their dad's antique Western Flyer, painted and polished and oiled and spoiled to perfect-o condition. Who wants to ride with the crowd?

Anyway, just checking in, E.D. I've got Grandpa's fresh blueberries and my mom's blueberry muffin recipe in my basket. Hope the Long kitchen has everything else.

I'm not nervous or anything, right? . . . So why do my legs feel like Jello and my stomach like a Boy Scout knot? They're only the kids of the principal of Hampton Falls Junior High, where I've got to spend the next couple of years of my life.

Here's the house . . . over and out.

— *Click!* —

Day 4,834 . . . a day of infamy in the Secret Adventures of Drea Thomas.

Well, E.D., it's over. I should have known I was in trouble when I walked into the house and saw a *computerized* "Invoice for Baby-sitting Services" from Arlene Blake lying on the desk by the front door.

My next clue was that the little kid—Matt—was not impressed with my Big Idea.

"Making muffins?" he protested when I brought out the blueberries and the recipe. "That's *girls'* stuff." Then he plopped down in a chair, folded his arms, and stuck out his six-year-old lip. "I'll eat 'em, but that's it."

I tried calling his bluff. "No cook 'em, no eat 'em," I said cheerfully, hunting in Mrs. Long's cupboards for flour and sugar.

"*Arlene* just fixes a snack for me to eat," Matt scowled. "She *never* makes me cook."

I happen to know that Arlene only baby-sat once—on trial, like me—but I was definitely playing second fiddle already.

So I tried a different tactic. "Okay, you don't have to cook," I said, "but could you run water over these blueberries?"

Bingo. What six-year-old can resist water play? While Matt knelt on a chair and happily blasted the blueberries with the sink sprayer, I started hunting for the rest of the muffin ingredients. That's when I realized that nine-year-old Rebecca was leaning against the kitchen doorway, arms crossed, just staring at me through her wire rims.

"Why do you wear such funny clothes?" she asked.

What a question! After all, I was just wearing my yellow and red chili-pepper vest and red bow tie. I thought kids liked that kind of stuff.

So I tried a question of my own. "Where does your mother keep the baking powder?" I asked her. I'd been through every cupboard twice and couldn't find it.

"We don't have any," Rebecca said, peering matter-of-factly at me through her wire rim glasses which make her look like a short sixteen-year-old instead of nine.

"What do you mean you don't have any? How do you know?" I asked. This was beginning to sound like a not-so-funny comedy.

"'Cause Mom never bakes anything. She's too busy working—you know, since Daddy died."

"Oh," I said. I knew Mrs. Long was a single mom, but I'd never really thought about why. Man, that would be really tough to lose your dad . . . I could hardly imagine it. But I looked at Rebecca with new respect. She and Matt must have been through a lot—their Mom, too.

"I'm really sorry . . . about your dad, I mean," I said. Rebecca just kinda shrugged and gave a little nod.

At that point my mind clicked over to emergency mode. It was time to get this show on the road. I stared at the recipe my mother had given me. *Four teaspoons baking powder*, it said. That wasn't so much, I thought—not compared to two-and-a-half cups flour and a cup of sugar. So maybe the baking powder wouldn't be missed.

"Maybe you could use this instead," Rebecca offered, handing me a box of baking soda.

Sounded like a bright idea. Mom makes substitutions all the time when she's cooking. "Good idea, Becky!" I said.

Rebecca jerked back the box of baking soda. "Don't call me Becky!" she said crossly. "My name is Rebecca. R-E-B-E-C-C-A."

See what I was up against, E.D.? Just call me Blunder Wonder—and I'd only been there half an hour.

But after crossing my heart and hoping to die twice that I'd never call Rebecca "Becky" again, we were ready for the blueberries.

That's when I realized I had totally forgotten about Matt, who by this time had not only thoroughly sprayed the blueberries but the wall, the counter, the floor, himself, and Floyd—that's the Long's hairy sheepdog, who looks sorta like a huge dustmop with teeth.

I squeezed my eyes shut. It was either time to have a nervous breakdown or . . . a Secret Adventure.

Why not? What could I lose? If these kids were like others I've baby-sat for, they'd be able to see my imagination, too. That's just the way kids are . . . they can't help it! It's infectious!

So I turned off the water, swooped Matt off the chair, and hissed in his ear, "Look, kid, just keep acting like everything's normal. But keep an eye on those blueberries . . . 'cause if they escape, we're in big trouble."

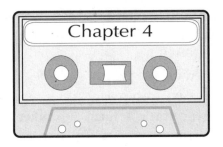

Hurricane Thomas
Hits the Long House

Matt stared at me curiously through his wet hair. "What do you mean, escape?"

"Shhh!" I said, grabbing Rebecca's hand and pulling both kids into the pantry. "Don't let 'em know we're onto them or the jig is up."

Rebecca looked at me like I was a talking teddy bear—as if wondering whether I was cute and harmless or just weird.

Matt peered around the corner of the pantry. "Why? What did they do?" he asked.

"What? Don't you know who these guys are?" I asked, incredulously. I dropped my voice again. "Ever hear of the California Raisins?"

"Of course," Rebecca said, tossing her head. "Everybody has." She turned to Matt. "You know that commercial . . . " and she started to hum, "'I heard it through the grape - vine . . .'"

Matt grinned. "Oh, yeah! But . . . what does that have to do with those blueberries?"

By this time I was whispering conspiratorially. "Well, these dudes are cousins of the California Raisins . . . but there the similarity ends. I mean, these are real bad dudes . . . the Blueberry Bums they call themselves. Something went down in Atlantic City, and I heard that these guys are trying to get to L.A. where they can get some sun, a few wrinkles, and blend in with the California Raisins and the surfing crowd . . . ya know, lay low for a while. And these dudes are slippery . . . why just the other day at my house, a bunch of 'em tried to escape. That's why I'm on my guard."

Matt was peeking around the pantry door at the colander of blueberries on the kitchen counter, when all of a sudden his eyes widened . . .

"Look, Drea!" he cried, pointing. "They're getting away!"

Sure enough, the dripping wet blueberries were making a break for it. Over the side of the colander they leaped, then slid along the wet counter and dropped like a waterfall onto the floor.

"Get 'em!" I yelled, making a dash from the pantry. "Don't let 'em get away!"

There was sudden pandemonium in the Long kitchen. The Blueberry Bums split up and rolled in a half dozen directions . . . under the table . . . into the corners . . . even right through our legs and into the pantry.

Floyd was barking madly at the rolling blue-berries as he slipped on the wet floor and tripped over his own paws.

In spite of herself, Rebecca got caught up in the excitement. "I got some cornered over here!" she yelled. I looked in her direction . . . she was nose to nose with a handful of blueber-ries who were backed up against a cupboard.

"Me, too!" yelled Matt. He scooped up a handful and stuffed them in his pants pocket, while he went after a few renegades who were rolling like crazy for the pantry.

"Man, we make a good team!" I crowed. Within minutes, Rebecca, Matt, and I had corralled all the Blueberry Bums and dumped them in a plastic bowl with a snap-on lid.

"What are we going to do with them now?" Matt asked, panting.

"Ah ha!" I said. "That's where the muffins come in. The only way to keep these guys from heading for L.A. and wrecking havoc on the West Coast is to bake 'em inside some blueberry muffins. That'll nip this little escape plot in the bud . . . here, Matt, you guard the blueberries . . . Rebecca, hand me that flour . . . now the sugar . . . eggs . . . milk . . . baking powder—oops, I mean baking soda substitute . . . there! Now we're ready for the blueberries. All right, Matt . . . when I count to three, you open the lid on the plastic bowl and dump them in here quick. Are you ready?"

Matt nodded eagerly.

"One . . . two . . . three!"

Matt lifted the lid and in one swoop poured the berries into the muffin batter.

"Wait!" cried Rebecca. "Two are getting away!"

Once again there was a mad dash . . . and while we were running after the two escapees, another five climbed out of the batter and tried to make a break for it. But the batter bogged them down, and soon all the blueberries were back in the bowl.

"We gotta work fast, guys," I urged. Rebecca

turned on the oven, while Matt put little muffin papers in the muffin pan. I quickly scooped spoonfuls of blueberry batter into the muffin papers and popped the pan into the oven, while Rebecca set the timer . . .

"Whew!" I sighed, dropping into a chair. "We did it! Good work, guys."

And then, as our Secret Adventure faded away, the three of us looked silently around the kitchen. It looked like Hurricane Thomas had just blown through. The counters and floor around the sink were still sopping wet where Matt had been spraying the blueberries . . . muffin batter was splattered all over the kitchen table . . . Floyd's footprints made a clear path through spilled flour dusting the floor . . . and an unmistakable blue stain was growing in the vicinity of Matt's pants pocket where he'd stuffed a few stray blueberries.

I was speechless.

"Uh oh," said Rebecca.

Matt looked pale as he stared at the stain on his pants. "Oh, no . . . Mom's gonna kill me." He looked wildly about. "We can tell her . . . we can tell her Floyd did it! And . . . and I'll put the pants in the garbage and she probably won't miss 'em for weeks!"

That's right! I thought frantically. *Hide the evidence!* But underneath I knew it wasn't right.

I finally found my voice. "I don't think so, Matt," I said, getting a wet paper towel and dabbing at the stain on his pants. Unfortunately, my dabbing only made it worse. "My Grandpa always says that 'the truth will come out.' It doesn't pay to cover things up. You always get found out in the end—and then it's even worse."

"Ahem . . . what could be worse than this?" said a voice. Startled, all three of us whirled around . . . and there was Mrs. Long, home early from the teachers' reception, standing in the kitchen doorway, surveying the chaos.

And in that moment, I knew it was good-bye baby-sitting job.

I tried to explain about making muffins and having some imaginary fun in the process and that we were just about to clean up . . . but then there was the blueberry stain . . .

My futile blabbing was interrupted by the cheerful DING! of the timer.

"Hey!" said Matt, grabbing a hot mitt. "The muffins are done!" With Rebecca's help, the two children proudly took the muffin tin out of the oven and set it on a hot pad on the counter . . . and then stared at it in astonishment.

"Why are they so flat?" Matt asked in a small voice.

Well, E.D., I was asking that question myself. Whatever was inside those little muffin papers was blueberry *something*, but they sure didn't look like any blueberry muffins I'd ever seen.

Matt gingerly took one of the papers out of the muffin tin and held it out for his mother. "Here, Mom," he said sadly. "We made these for you."

I almost laughed . . . this was the same little boy who a couple hours ago had crossed his arms stubbornly and said baking muffins was "girls' stuff." But I didn't laugh, because Mrs. Long was actually peeling the paper off and taking a bite of the flat little pancake.

Mrs. Long chewed about twice, and then a strange look crossed her face. Stepping gingerly across the flour-and-water covered floor, she grabbed a paper towel and spit the muffin into it.

"Uh . . . what exactly did you put in these muffins?" she asked, trying not to gag.

What was that I'd said to Matt about "the truth will always come out"? "Er . . . the missing baking powder must have been more important than I gave it credit for," I sighed.

And so the whole story came out. We spent the next half hour washing the floor and the table and the counters and even Floyd's paws. Then Mrs. Long sent Matt to change his pants. I expected her to be really mad about the ruined pants, but all she said was, "Next time you run into a berry stain, Drea, try boiling water."

Guess you learn new things every day, E.D.

Only it was too late for me. I knew I'd blown this baby-sitting job *big time*.

Mrs. Long insisted on paying me, even though I said I didn't deserve it because of Matt's ruined pants and the mess we made in the kitchen. But that money sure felt heavy in my pocket as I pedaled my bike home.

So that's it . . . my brief career baby-sitting for the principal's kids is over—zilch—zero—out. I laughed at Kimberly's prediction about getting permanent detention if I messed up—remember? Well, E.D., I'm not laughing any more.

Over and out—in more ways than one.

— *Click!* —

It's Day 4,835, the day after the babysitting fiasco, and you're not gonna believe this, E.D.! I'm still pinching myself to make sure I'm not inside one of my own Secret Adventures. Mrs. Long called this afternoon and offered me the regular after-school baby-sitting job! I was so flabbergasted that I barely heard her say why—something about Matt begging for me to baby-sit again, and she appreciated me being honest even about the things that had gone wrong. "We all learn from our mistakes, Drea," she said. "And I promise to buy some baking powder."

"But what about Arlene Blake?" I said. "I mean, she's got those business cards, and . . . and invoices, and everything."

Mrs. Long laughed. "Oh, she's very organized, no doubt about it . . . *and* very neat." I groaned inside, but she went on. "But the person I'm looking for is someone who enjoys being with kids, puts energy into doing things with them, and takes responsibility, even when things end up in a bit of a mess."

I'm still in shock. I got the job! I'm telling you first, E.D., but now I gotta call Kimberly. She is *not* going to believe this.

— Click! —

Back again, E.D. Kimberly raved about my great news—although I suspect she was more glad that I beat out Arlene than that I got the job. And she gave me a hard time about baby-sitting for the principal, of all people.

"Guess that makes me an FOB—Friend of Baby-sitter," she told me. (Okay, it's a lame joke, but ya know, like "FOB—Friend of Bill" . . . Bill Clinton, the President, that is.)

But I know at least one person who is not going to be amused at my good fortune. Kimberly might be an FOB, but as of this moment, I'm sure I'm the Number One EOA . . . Enemy of Arlene.

— Click! —

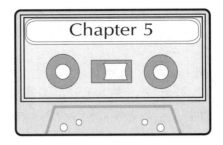

Chapter 5

Big Tubas and Little Toasters

It's . . . wait, where's my watch . . . Day 4,851 in the Secret Adventures of Drea Thomas, and boy, am I late—but there's Mom, right on time, yelling up the stairs that I'm going to be late for school.

I was right—an electronic diary is easier than writing all of this stuff down . . . at least I can talk while I'm getting ready for school . . . uh! where's my other saddle shoe? Oh, there it is . . .

Anyway. You wouldn't believe how my dad woke me up this morning, E.D. *Blasting* on his sousaphone right outside my door, that's what. And then he insisted on playing a tuba version of reveille—just because I overslept till 7:30. Why can't he wake me up like other parents?

Still, it's a good thing he did, because Kimberly wanted to meet me at school early today. "Critical," she said. But then, *everything's* critical to Kimberly.

Okay, time for the book bag check. History book . . . mirror . . . Kimberly's earrings that I borrowed . . . homework . . . brush . . . notebooks . . . check, check, check . . .

Only one prob with an electronic diary, E.D. I mean, what if I become famous some day and a future historian has to *transcribe* all of this? Oh, well, not to worry—not if my future greatness is anything like my present popularity. It's like the really popular kids in junior high—Arlene Blake and her crowd—are in a different league . . .

Not that I'm *un*popular now . . . after all, can't you hear my name being yelled over and over from the first floor? Ignore the fact that it sounds like my mom.

Enough for now . . . My "fans" are calling . . . this is Drea Thomas saying, "Good-bye to the past, hello to the future!" . . . Hey, I like that!

— Click! —

 Place: kitchen. *Time:* 7:46. Not bad for getting out of bed at 7:30!

That brunette blur was my mom going out the door to her job at Jamison's department store. The store's new ad campaign came out in the *Hampton*

Falls Sentinel today, but she didn't look too happy . . . she said Old Man Jamison wrote it himself: "Jamison's—Your Store of Stores"—or something like that.

When I came down a few minutes ago, she was sitting at the kitchen table dressed in a nice cream and tan pantsuit, finishing her coffee, and gazing mournfully at the new ad in the newspaper.

"If you don't like it," I said, "why don't you change it? After all, Mom, you're Jamison's head honcho of marketing."

"Wish it was that easy," she said, rolling her eyes. "Actually, my job requirement is to make everyone love it."

I know that out there in the dog-eat-dog corporate world, my mom is Laurie Thomas, tough marketing executive. And besides that, she's a great mom who dispenses more than the minimum daily requirement of hugs and TLC . . . as well as being just crazy enough to appreciate my dad. But I couldn't let her get away with thinking *she's* the only one with "job requirements."

"Face it, Mom," I told her, "your job requirements are a piece of cake compared to the ones we kids have. Could *you* memorize every known fact about George Washington, our beloved and super-honest first president of the good ol' U.S. of A.?"

Mom was not impressed. "Take seventh grade over again? No, thanks! I'd probably get stuck doing a report on Ben Franklin—he's the guy who wanted the *turkey* to be our national bird instead of the eagle." She made a face. "And it'd be my assignment to make everyone think it was a great idea!"

Ha. Knowing my mom, she'd have everybody believing that the turkey should be on the endangered species list and every patriotic citizen would eat pizza with pepperoni for Thanksgiving.

Anyway . . . Mom's gone and I've got two minutes to get something to eat and blast myself outta here. A piece of toast oughta do it . . .

I stuck a piece of bread into our old 1952 Sunbeam toaster and looked real close at my reflection to check out a pimple that had just taken up residence on my face . . . and laughed as my nose became large and rounded in the shiny chrome. In a blink, I was face to face with my friend Mr. Toaster. I punched down the handle . . .

"Ouch," said the toaster. "Careful there. I'm a little sensitive from that stale English muffin you tried to toast yesterday."

"'Mornin', Toaster," I grinned,

greeting my imaginary friend, who now sported a Jimmy Durante bulbous nose.

"Hmmm. That's MISTER Toaster to you, toots," huffed the toaster.

"Everybody's so uptight this morning," I moaned, waiting impatiently for the toast. "What's the deal?"

"How many forty-year-old talking toasters do you know that are cheerful in the morning?" Mister Toaster shuddered as his wires heated up. "Ohhhh . . . I think I just sprained a spring." The toaster raised a bushy eyebrow. "So, what are you still doing here anyway? Weren't you supposed to meet Kimberly at 7:45 at school?"

I thought the toast was gonna pop up, but it was only the toaster ringing up the time like a cash register: ding! 7:45!

"Whoa . . . thanks for reminding me." I grabbed my brown leather book bag and jammed my black "Forties" hat on my head.

"No problem," said Mister Toaster. "Perfect timing is a part of any good toaster's training . . . that and what to do when some dummy puts a knife in your slots." Sparks flew as a jolt of electricity crackled inside the toaster. "Yowwww! Ouchhhhhh! Neverrrr put anything metal in aaaaa toasterrrrr."

Boy, where do these ideas come from, E.D.? One

minute I'm talking to a grumpy toaster, and the next I'm standing face to face with a burnt piece of toast! Well, forget the toast. I gotta jet—

Oh, hi, Dad. Uh . . . wouldn't it be easier getting through the kitchen door if you took off that overgrown tuba? . . . 'Bye, Dad—gotta meet Kimberly.
                    — *Click!* —

I'm gonna try something, E.D.—see if I can keep recording and ride my bike at the same time. Testing . . . testing . . . okay, guess this is gonna work.

Anyway, picking up where I left off.

Dad came in the kitchen just as I was leaving and I said, "'Bye, Dad—gotta meet Kimberly," and Dad said, "Kimberly? Kimberly who? Is she someone I've seen around here before?"

Honestly, E.D.! He's not very funny. "Yes, Dad," I said, trying not to roll my eyes, "only for the last thirteen years. Can't you cut her some slack?"

"I've tried, I've tried," he said, "but she speaks some form of alien slang. Can't you find a best friend who's an earthling?"

This from a man wearing suspenders and a big, brass tuba around his neck! But I decided to humor him.

"I'm in junior high, Dad. Everyone's pretty much extraterrestrial." Good point, don't you think, E.D.?

Anyway, we are now leaving the Thomas driveway . . . I can still hear Dad practicing his "Sonata for Sousaphone" for the Tuba Festival next week at the college . . . hmmm. I wonder if that means I have to call him my "Oomph-Pa-Pa"? . . .

If I had a video camera instead of a Walkman, I could show our house. . . . It's a pretty neat house—sorta Victorian style I guess, gray and white, with a large front porch and a balcony above the porch . . . there's my attic room up under the eaves facing the front . . .

Now I'm riding my bike down the tree-shaded streets of Hampton Falls, New Jersey. Guess it's a pretty typical college town . . . you can see the ancient spires on campus towering over the trees . . . the small, exclusive shops are downtown, surrounded by older houses and the park, with housing developments and shopping malls pushing out the fringes, creating our very own suburban sprawl. But guess being a hip college town isn't enough . . . last year the city council wanted to promote our town as a great place to live, so they came up with the slogan, "Hampton Falls—Bookbinding Capital of the Atlantic Seaboard!" But honestly, E.D., three bookbinding companies is hardly a claim to fame—whoaaa!

Rebecca and Matt! I almost ran into you!

— *Click!* —

47

Well, E.D., that may be one of the little hazards of trying to ride my bike and record my electronic diary at the same time. I almost ran into Rebecca and Matt Long, which would *definitely* not be good for my babysitting reputation. They were on their way to school, and Matt, of course, was wearing his favorite blue baseball cap with the red brim.

But get this . . . Rebecca was making Matt walk several paces behind her—"Because," she explained to me primly, "he's just realized his lifelong dream of walking to school without stepping on a crack in the sidewalk." Then when Matt ran up and gave me a hug, she gleefully pointed out that he had just stepped on a crack .

"Did not!" Matt yelled back at her.

"Did too!"

"Liar."

"Double liar."

I could tell this was getting nowhere. "Hey, give it a rest," I said. "I'll see you after school, okay?" On the days I baby-sit, they come straight to my house because it's right down the street from the elementary school . . . though today I wouldn't be surprised if they came by different sidewalks.

This is only the third week I've been baby-sitting for Mrs. Long, and I'm still getting to know the kids. Rebecca's okay—when she's not informing me that she's too old for a baby-sitter. Matt's a

riot—I think he sleeps with that baseball cap on!—
but I think he's having a tough time adjusting to
first grade. Not to mention the fact that his older
sister sometimes treats him like dirt . . .

Hampton Falls Junior High straight ahead. The
time is . . . 7:59. Fourteen minutes late meeting
Kimberly—she's going to kill me. Wonder why she
wanted to meet me early? There's George, locking
up his bike at the bike rack. Guess this is where I
sign off, E.D. . . .

— Click! —

Man . . . If I'd known what I was walking into
when I got to school today, E.D., I would have
turned around on my Western Flyer and called in
sick . . .

It's after school now. I just got home, and the
Long kids will be here any minute, but I'll try to get
started. Guess I'll pick up where I left off, when I
saw George locking up his snazzy mountain bike at
the bike rack this morning . . .

He said, "Yo, Drea!" in that cool way he has. No,
my heart did not skip a beat . . . after all, George and
I have been friends since first grade. Good friends,
yes, but, really, nothing more.

"Hey, George, what'zappin-ing?" I said.

"Everything's zappin-ing!" George said, frown-
ing at me. "Did Kimberly fill you in on this election
thing yet? Kimberly, Bobby, and I—some others,

too—think that *no way* should Arlene Blake run unopposed for seventh grade class president. It's undemocratic!"

I shrugged. "Yeah, but nobody in their right mind would run against Miss Popularity."

"What about you?" he said.

"Very funny," I told him. What does he think . . . that I've got applesauce for brains?

"But think about all that stuff we've been learning in U.S. History class, Drea," he said. "What would G. Washington say if he caught wind of an unopposed election at Hampton Falls Junior High? He'd be bummed."

I knew where this was leading, so I shook my head vigorously. "Sorry, but no way. Arlene Blake would like nothing better than to totally smear me in an election campaign. Don't you remember? I'm already hugely on Arlene's blacklist for 'stealing' the Long kids baby-sitting gig."

George shrugged. "Well, catch ya later, Drea, . . . but I still don't think Arlene ought to run for prez of the seventh grade unopposed."

As George headed for a bunch of his friends, I heard someone else calling my name . . . Kimberly, of course, smashing as usual in a red print jumper and red-and-white striped top.

"Drea Thomas! Finally!" she scolded. "You call this *early*? . . . Never mind." Kimberly grabbed my arm and dragged me toward the front door of the school. "C'mon. I've found the absolute-a-mundo primo person to crush the Arlene Machine!"

Well, good, I thought innocently. Then maybe Kimberly would get off my back and George would get his wish. Frankly, I didn't really care who this "absolute-a-mundo primo person" was—just so there'd be a choice and I wouldn't actually have to *vote* for Arlene myself.

. . . Uh-oh. There's the doorbell. That's probably Rebecca and Matt, so guess I'll have to pick this up later.

But I tell you one thing, E.D., I wasn't prepared for what I saw when I walked through those doors . . .

Over and out till later.

— Click! —

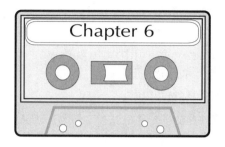

Drea All the Way-A!

Back again, E.D. It's still Day 4,851 ... but Mrs. Long just picked up Rebecca and Matt ... something kinda weird happened while they were here, but I'll get to that later. First I gotta tell you what happened at school today. Now where was I? ... Guess I better run the tape backwards to see where I left off ...

— Click! —

Oh, right ... Kimberly and I were standing on the front steps of the school.

"Close your eyes!" she demanded.

"Why?" I asked. "Where are we going?"

"Just close 'em," she said.

So I sighed and closed my eyes. Honestly, E.D., humoring Kimberly sometimes makes me feel like a dork.

I let her drag me into the hallway and the next thing I knew Kimberly was saying, "Okay, Drea, open 'em up. *Tah-dah!*"

I opened my eyes . . . and instantly went into major shock—at least an 8.6 on the Richter Scale of disasters.

The walls of the hallway had disappeared. Instead of institutional green paint, all I could see were hundreds—maybe thousands—of posters with my name on them.

DREA FOR 7TH GRADE PRESIDENT!

WITH DREA—ALL THE WAY-A!

NO DOUBTS ABOUT THOMAS—VOTE FOR DREA!

A-OKAY-A WITH DREA!

When I finally found my voice, I hissed, "Kimberly Andow! What is all this? I said, no—N-O—I didn't want to run."

"No, you didn't," she smiled sweetly. "I distinctly remember you said you'd think about it. So . . . what do you think about it?"

I opened my mouth to give Kimberly a piece of my mind, but was practically jerked off my feet as my so-called best friend . . . *best friend???* Who needs enemies with a best friend like Kimberly! Anyway . . . as Kimberly pulled me down the hallway.

"Before you answer," Kimberly said seriously, "let's put this in perspective. One: Arlene represents the 'popular' kids, and *someone* needs to personify all the hardworking schlubs and schlubettes around here. . . . Two: someone needs to run against Arlene and you are by far the best candidate. Just ask George and Bobby. . . . Three: it will look great on your permanent school record. . . . And four: with me as your campaign manager, you can't lose!"

Well, she certainly had her speech well prepared. I again had just opened my mouth to protest when she poked me in the ribs.

"Chill, *mon candidat*," she said, "here comes the competition."

Sure enough, Arlene Blake and her shadow, Marcy Mannington, were walking deliberately toward Kimberly and me until they were in-your-face close. I could even smell Arlene's spearmint-flavored mouthwash.

"Well, *Andrea*," said Arlene, gesturing toward the deluge of campaign posters. "I see you've been your usual busy self."

I decided to ignore the fact that she called me

Andrea. "Look, Arlene . . . this really wasn't my idea," I told her.

But Arlene certainly wasn't in a mood to believe me. "Don't play innocent with me, Drea Thomas," she said, narrowing those big eyes of hers. "If you want to run against me for president of the seventh grade, at least have the guts to tell me to my face." Then she tossed back that golden mane. "Of course," she went on, "no one will vote for you. You'll just embarrass yourself in front of the whole school."

"Yeah," Marcy chimed in. The Shadow was enjoying this.

"Besides," Arlene continued, "you're not going to *luck* into this one like you did with that cheap baby-sitting stunt with Mrs. Long's kids."

I was just about to tell Arlene that it was all a mistake and I wasn't running for class prez . . . but that comment about "cheap baby-sitting stunt" was too much. "Luck? Cheap baby-sitting stunt?" I said. "*Excuse me*, Arlene. I thought that Mrs. Long *chose* me over you."

"Wrong," she sneered. "That little pea-brain son of hers chose you." . . .

That did it! Suddenly I felt like a mad gunslinger with a scratchy beard who hadn't had a bath in weeks . . . facin' down my arch enemy, Slick Arlie Blake. I squinted into the noonday sun and hitched up my gun belt. My throat was

57

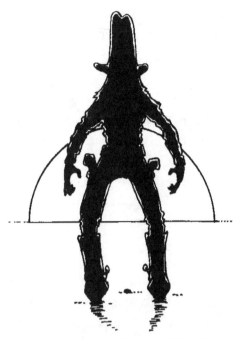

parched, making my voice gruff as I snarled, "Them's fightin' words, Slick Arlie." . . . Somewhere a horse whinnied, and I vaguely wondered how I got stuck in a bad "B" movie.

. . . Fighting words is right, E.D.! I couldn't let Arlene get away with calling Matt Long names.

"Let's correct a few things, Arlene Blake," I said indignantly. "One, Matt Long is not a pea brain—he's very intelligent. Two, he has great taste in baby-sitters. And three, if you are running your campaign anything like this ridiculous conversation, then there is only going to be one embarrassed candidate Friday . . . and it won't take a genius to figure out who that is!"

Now it was Marcy's turn to look shocked. No one *ever* talked to Arlene like that. It was junior high suicide.

Arlene's perfect summer tan turned two shades redder. "Eewww!!" she screeched. "You've just declared war, Drea Thomas. We'll just see who has what it takes to be elected class president!"

With that, the golden-haired goddess turned and stalked over to her locker, followed closely by The Shadow. To my relief, the first bell rang just then, scattering the spectators.

Kimberly gave me a "thumb's up." "*Yes.* We can beat her, Drea," she crowed happily.

By that time my shock had turned to fierce determination. "Right," I agreed.

Just then Mrs. Long came down the hall on her way to the principal's office. "Oh, Drea," she said, "glad to see that you're running for class president. I'm sure you will bring some unique insights to our student government." And then she was gone.

Kimberly looked at me with a smug smile. "See? This is incredible! In less than ten minutes, you've already become the second most popular girl in seventh grade!"

Still . . . it took me until second period to realize what I'd done, E.D. And by that time it was too late to back out . . .

Gotta finish this later, E.D. . . . I hear Dad calling me for supper. But believe me—there's more!

— *Click!* —

 Back again. Grandpa was over for dinner and wanted to play my old Nintendo games after we finished eating, so I made him a deal: I'd play him a game if he'd help me with the dishes. Pretty good deal, don't you think?

Anyway . . . back to school. It was crazy. During lunch period there was a long line of awe-struck boys in the hallway, waiting to get eight-by-ten copies of Arlene's school picture which she was signing. I don't think it was any accident that she was signing those pictures by the school *trophy case*, either . . .

As I was staring at the Hampton Falls Junior High trophy case, the rows upon rows of shiny, brass athletic trophies all seemed to melt and change shape, until each one had been remolded in the likeness of a different seventh-grade boy . . . tall

*ones, short ones, cute ones, plain ones, fat ones,
skinny ones—all grinning hypnotically. I peered
closer at the little plaques on the bottom of the
trophies. Each one read: "I voted for Arlene."*

Then I blinked, and all the trophies popped back
into their original soccer and basketball contortions.
"I'm starting to get paranoid," I muttered to myself.

But by sixth period I noticed that several of my
posters had mysteriously disappeared—not that
they really compared with Arlene's slick professional posters, some of which even looked
airbrushed. But later Kimberly told me that Bobby
saw Marcy stuffing a bunch of my posters in the
trash. Can you believe it, E.D.? How low can you
get?

Between periods, Kimberly made me stand in
the hall shaking hands and asking kids to vote for
me . . . which was pretty pathetic, considering that
for every student who shook my hand, there were
five around Arlene and Marcy, who were feeding
quarters into the soft drink machine and handing
out sodas in exchange for promises to vote for her.

The crowning touch was after school, when
Arlene appeared with a soccer ball and wearing a
Hampton Falls Soccer jersey, standing in front of a
sign that said, "Use Your Head . . . Vote for Arlene."
The nerve, E.D.! Arlene would never be caught
dead working up a sweat on the soccer field. But all

the guys were acting like she was their soccer mascot or something.

And George told somebody, who told Kimberly, who told me, that he overheard Arlene telling Marcy, "I'm going to pulverize that Drea Thomas. I don't care what you have to do, Marcy—but I'm not going to let that girl beat me again!" . . .

George and Bobby Wilson were waiting for me at the bike rack when I came out of school. Bobby— who's proud of his African-American heritage and "modestly" insists that he is Michael Jordan's third cousin twice removed—has been George's best buddy ever since the two of them discovered soccer in fifth grade. And since he's the school's star soccer player, no one dares challenge his dubious claim to famous relatives.

Anyway. I must have looked pretty down in the mouth, because they did their best to cheer me up.

"So you did it, Drea!" George said. "You decided to run."

"Yeah! Congratulations," said Bobby.

I tried to smile but it wasn't easy. "Yeah, well, it wasn't exactly intentional," I admitted. "It just kinda happened—thanks to you-know-who, who is suddenly the world's most enthusiastic campaign manager."

"Well, what you need now is a *spin* on your campaign platform," George said, as I unlocked my Western Flyer. "You know, a twist to the issues that sets you apart from Arlene."

"Issues?" I said. "I don't think Arlene has any issues. She's banking on being popular, pretty, and buying votes until her allowance runs out. You know, the things that *really* count." I was being sarcastic, of course. But still, those are probably the things that attract the typical voter—and are going to count me out.

"Exactly," said George, always the optimist. "So if you focus your campaign on the important things . . . you know, like character, and honesty . . ."

"And throw in some things like a student lounge," Bobby added.

That gave me an idea—what George said, I mean. "Hmm. I like that," I said. "Honesty would be a good spin. Sorta like ol' G. Washington himself."

"Got him elected," George agreed, flashing that amazing grin of his. I didn't want to correct him, but Miss Roth says G.W. got elected because he was a war hero and everyone hated John Adams . . . but I decided to go along.

"Well, thanks, guys," I told them, pushing off on my bike. "I appreciate the support."

"Who said we're going to vote for you?" Bobby yelled after me. "I'm still holding out for the student lounge!"

How do you like that, E.D.? Great guys. Loyal to the end . . . still, what they said made sense. I'll

never beat Arlene the way things are going now . . .
I need a *spin*, like George said, that sets me apart
from her . . . and the student lounge would be a nice
perk.

Anyway. As I said before, something kind of
funny happened when Rebecca and Matt came over
after school . . . but right now guess I better sign off
and hit the books so I don't *flunk* out of the election.

Over and out. I'll check in after my homework's
done.

— Click! —

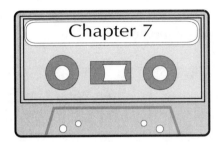

Maestro's Missing Music

Say, E.D., did you know a lot of people think that George Washington had wooden dentures? The actual fact is, he owned five sets of false teeth—including one made out of pigs' teeth!—but not one of them was wooden. Still . . . poor Martha!

However, if I cram one more fact in my head for the U.S. history test on Friday, my brain is going to split open and then I'll have a real mess to clean up! Still . . . that might be less of a mess than I've gotten myself into with this election thing, E.D.

Back to this afternoon when the Long kids arrived after school . . .

When Rebecca and Matt heard that I was running for class president at their mom's school, they immediately wanted to "help." So I dug up some poster paper and tempera paints and they set to work on the kitchen table making campaign posters for me.

They mean well, E.D., but after seeing the slick way Arlene is going after votes, I'm not sure a bunch of amateur posters begging, "Vote for Drea . . . Please?" are going to help me. Matt painted his heart out and held up his masterpiece—a blotchy picture of a dinosaur (I think) with the words, "Drea is Dino-Mite!" It was really cute . . . and I felt bad that it didn't cheer me up.

I keep thinking about what George said—about needing a *spin* on the election that would set me apart from Arlene. But frankly, I don't think anybody cares about "issues." This whole thing is about popularity.

But I didn't want to get too depressed while Matt and Rebecca were here, so I decided it was time to make a Drea Special for their snack—a tropical fruit milk shake. But what's a tropical snack without a little tropical music? It was time to let my imagination go and have a little FUN! . . .

First, we needed a little rhythm . . . so I snapped my fingers and there were the congas!
(Dah-da, dah-da, da—DA!)
Snap! Add some trumpets!
(Dah-da, dah-da, da—DA!)

All RIGHT! It was dancing music . . . couldn't help it, had ta move my feet . . . snap those castanets . . . I was beginning to feel like Hampton Falls' answer to Gloria Estafan!

"Okay, kids," I said, "what can we find in the 'fridge and fruit basket? . . . hmmm, half-gallon of milk . . . couple of bananas . . . some end-of-season strawberries . . . a fat pear . . . all right, Matt! Where'd you find those marshmal-lows? Doesn't matter . . . line 'em up there on the counter. First we gotta pour some milk into the blender, and . . . hit it, rhythm section!"

(Dah-da, dah-da, da—DA!)
(Dah-da, dah-da, da—DA!)

Suddenly the fruit began getting into the mood. The bananas were standing up tall and not-so-straight and dancing across the counter, followed by a conga line of strawberries, the pear, and hip marshmallows . . .

(Dah-da, dah-da, da—DA!)
(Dah-da, dah-da, da—DA!)

Across the counter they bobbed and hopped . . . up the stack of cookbooks . . . a whole line of dancing fruit parading to a Latin beat . . .

(Dah-da, dah-da, da—DA!)
(Dah-da, dah-da, da—DA!)

"And now, kids," I announced, "for a fantastic finale . . . watch those bananas, strawberries, the pear, and marshmallows all dive into the blender with a SPLASH . . ."

"OLE!" I cried, and turned on the blender, reducing milk and fruit to a delicious fruity slush.

Matt's eyes sparkled. "Man, if you campaigned like that at school, you'd be sure to win!"

"Sure would get people's attention," Rebecca added.

"Yeah . . . but," I reminded them, "so far only the kids I baby-sit for are able to see my imagination, remember?"

Matt looked pleased. "Oh. I forgot," he said.

While we were drinking our milk shakes, Dad came into the kitchen wearing—you guessed it,

E.D.—that overgrown tuba. "Hi, folks," he grinned, waving some music sheets, "just passing through campaign headquarters."

Now, you gotta understand about parents, E.D. They're always "passing through" or "just coming in to get something." It's their way of checking up on how things are going without looking nosy. Nice try, but I've been on to this little gimmick since I was in diapers.

But this time Dad's grin didn't match his forehead, which was all wrinkled and worried. "Has anybody seen a stack of my composition sheets?" he asked. "I laid them down somewhere, but I don't remember where . . . and now I've lost the whole second movement of my Sonata for Sousaphone!"

Personally, I didn't think it would hurt to lose the whole thing . . . but Dad was really serious and I felt sorry for him. So I looked around on all the kitchen counters, and even in the wastebasket, but didn't see any music sheets. I asked Matt and Rebecca if they'd seen anything when they first got here, but they both said no. Poor Dad . . . he went wandering off muttering, "*Where* could I have put them?"

Hang on a minute, E.D. . . . I'm gonna get in my pajamas before I finish this . . .

— *Click!* —

... Okay, I'm back. That's better. There's nothing like wrapping yourself in flannel and a warm blanket to give the illusion that all's well with the world. But all is *not* well in my corner of the universe ... at least if Kimberly's right. You see, E. D., the phone rang while the kids were cleaning up their paints and poster stuff ...

I answered the kitchen phone with my best phone manners: "Sherwood Forest, Maid Marion speaking."

It was Kimberly. "I've got news for you," she said. "We're *way* down in the polls."

"What polls?!" I asked. Then I realized it was just Kimberly in her starring role as campaign manager. "Whatever . . . ," I muttered. "We better face it—we're going to get creamed."

"*Au contraire, mon Drare!*" she cried. "We can still win with the 'spin' that your brilliant campaign manager—*moi*—has come up with . . ."

Maybe she's been talking to George, I thought.

". . . I suggest that we figure out a way to use Arlene's own tactics against her," Kimberly went on. "Arlene may have duped Marcy Mannington into being her campaign manager, but Marcy's no match for Yours Truly."

No argument there. But I wasn't sure what this new "spin" was that Kimberly had in mind . . . it didn't exactly sound like the G.W. thing George was pushing.

"We've only got one more day before the election," I reminded her desperately. "We've got to find a way to really impact the voters. They need to know what the issues are! George and Bobby said . . ."

"Absolutely," she interrupted. "We've got to let the Arlene Machine know that Drea Thomas is a candidate not to be messed with."

"All I know," I said, "is that tomorrow we're in an all-out race for the finish line. But that's not a lot of time to establish a campaign theme—you know, like honesty and character. And," I added, "we need a tempting campaign promise, like the student lounge idea of Bobby's."

"Great idea! Not to worry, Drea. We still have enough time to let Arlene and Marcy know that we're gonna give 'em a fight they'll never forget!"

Maybe Kimberly's right, E.D. Arlene's a tough candidate to beat and we're going to have to fight for every vote. All I know is, what happens in the next two days could change my whole life . . . well, at least this school year, anyway.

Oh . . . one more thing. Matt acted kinda strange all afternoon—real quiet. And when Mrs. Long came to pick up the kids, he didn't even say goodbye to me . . . just shot out the door like a rocket. Seemed kinda funny . . . hope it wasn't the milk shake. Oh, well. Guess I've got a lot to learn about moody first graders.

G'night, E.D. Over and out.

— *Click!* —

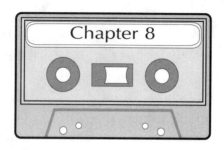

Come Out Swingin'

Gonna try my electronic diary on the way to school again, E.D.—see if I can do this and ride my bike at the same time without sending me or some unfortunate jogger to the hospital . . .

Poor Dad. I was up this morning before he got to blast me with his tuba version of reveille. I think he was really disappointed I wasn't late again.

It's . . . Day 4,852 in the Secret Adventures of Drea Thomas—alias Dark Horse Candidate for Seventh Grade Class President. Decided to wear my bright blue necktie today and melon-colored hat . . . something cheerful to keep my spirit up.

Got to the kitchen in time to actually have breakfast. This morning I was determined to outwit the toaster and pop my toast up *before* it turned into a charcoal frisbee. But then, I wasn't counting on Mr. Toaster having a few ideas of his own . . .

As I entered the kitchen, I was greeted by none other than Mr. Toaster—sporting a press badge in one of his slots! "Why, it looks like . . . yes, ladies and gentlemen, pots and pans, it's Drea Thomas—the next seventh grade president of Hampton Falls Junior High!" he cackled.

Suddenly the toaster's side handle transformed into a reporter's microphone which he stuck in my face. "Drea, do you have a statement for the kitchen?"

Statement? Mr. Toaster wanted an interview at 7:15 in the morning? What about my breakfast! But . . . I rolled my eyes and patiently answered—after all, I am a political candidate who is responsible to my voting public. "Well, yes," I said, "we do have a new approach. My campaign manager assures me we will win, even with a late start."

I gave Mr. Toaster my best media smile and turned toward the news on the little kitchen TV. There was something familiar about that news-

caster shuffling his papers . . . he was looking straight at the camera . . . no, he was looking straight at me!

"Excuse me, Drea," said the voice from the TV. "John Tesh here from Hollywood. Arlene Blake was assured of victory yesterday at Hampton Falls Junior High. What's different today?"

Ah, the wonders of the electronic media! Two-way TV! Instant publicity! Well, it sure couldn't hurt!

I quickly straightened my tie for the camera. "Well, two things are different," I answered, thinking fast. "One, I've been conducting a detailed study of George Washington, our first president, and I want to embody his sense of honesty in my campaign. And two, I intend to bring my campaign a higher visibility."

John Tesh's blue eyes seemed to pierce the electronic screen. "Aren't you fooling yourself by thinking this new approach will benefit the student body? In truth, won't you become just like the other candidate, determined to win at all costs?"

Uh . . . this little interview wasn't going quite the way I'd like. "Of course not!" I protested. "Neither Kimberly nor I would ever do anything wrong or unfair . . ."

"Well, of course you wouldn't, Sweetheart," my mom's voice broke into my imaginary interview. I looked at the TV, and John Tesh was talking about the spin on U2's latest record tour.

I blinked and tried to focus on my mom, who was standing in the kitchen doorway with a pleased smile on her face. She looked pretty as usual in a light blue blazer and navy skirt. But that's not what really caught my eye. It was the white apron she was holding up for me to see, which said in bright red letters: JAMISON'S—YOUR STORE OF STORES.

"Well, what do you think?" she asked. "Tempting free gift for the mom on the go?"

I couldn't imagine wearing it myself—but, hey, there's no accounting for people's tastes. One day on the campaign trail had already taught me that people will take anything—as long as it's free. "Sure," I told her, giving her an encouraging smile. "Looks like your campaign strategy is going better than mine."

"Relax, honey," she said, giving me a peck on the cheek. "You're going to be fine." Then she

grabbed her briefcase and was out the door before she heard Dad calling her name.

"She's gone, Dad!" I yelled back. He appeared in the kitchen wearing . . . DA TUBA, of course, but his hair was all wild like he'd been running his hands through it.

"I *still* can't find my Tuba Sonata!" he said. I could see the situation was getting desperate. He thumped the kitchen table and said, "I thought I put it down right here . . . but who knows? Could you ask Matt and Rebecca again if they saw anything yesterday?"

I promised. After all, those kids are masters at finding lost things—especially Matt. Personally, I think he's been living with El Doggo Floyd, for so long, that he sniffs things out like a bloodhound . . .

Well, there's the junior high up ahead and I'm still in one piece and so are the lucky joggers along my bike route. Guess I'm getting the knack of yakking on wheels.

Anyway. Wish me luck, E.D. Yesterday I walked innocently through those doors and found myself dragged into a campaign showdown with Arlene Blake. Today is the day before the election and the campaign enters a new round—and my guess is that Kimberly will come out swinging! I can hear the fight bell now!

— *Click!* —

It's still Day 4,852, now seventeen-hundred hours (that's five o'clock, ya know) ... Rebecca and Matt have come and gone and I'm sitting out here on the second floor balcony of our house. Something just happened with Matt that I need time to think about . . . but first, maybe I should back up and fill you in on what else happened today, E.D.

I got to school early, and Kimberly had made a lot of "Vote for Drea" tags for kids to wear—although black marker on self-adhesive labels looked pretty pathetic next to the "Arlene Is Keen" campaign buttons Marcy was handing out. Still, I appreciated Kimberly's effort.

Then on my way to first period class, I saw that someone had drawn a black mustache on Arlene's picture on some of her posters. It looked really funny . . . and I caught myself thinking, *Serves her right for being so vain.* Not that *I* would ever deface someone else's poster, E.D. . . . but, hey! what could I do if my supporters got a little out of hand, right?

At lunchtime, things heated up a little . . . well, a lot. As I came out of the lunchroom, Kimberly was standing in the hallway loudly calling out her latest campaign scoops. "Arlene Blake supports animal testing . . . and she's against any rain forest policy . . . Arlene also wants the New Jersey Nets to move to Baltimore . . ."

Now, E.D., I don't know where Kimberly got

her facts, but if that's what Arlene thinks, the voters have a right to know. Right?

At least Kimberly was starting to draw a crowd—which is more than I can say when I was trying to talk to kids about "the issues" yesterday. Just as I got there, Kimberly was saying, "Drea Thomas wants to create a new student lounge, but Arlene has gone on record as not supporting that idea."

Just then an extremely mad voice said, "I have not!" All heads turned as Arlene pushed her way to the front of the crowd, followed closely by The Shadow, of course. Arlene looked like a cover girl on *Seventeen*, as usual—black two-piece suit with the mandatory short skirt and white tights.

Anyway . . . Kimberly was quick. "*Exactly*!" she said. "You have not supported an idea that would create a place where all students could meet. Drea Thomas won't stand for that . . . or for your earth-damaging environmental policy!"

"My *what*?" Arlene exploded.

I felt a little uncomfortable with what was happening, but it *was* kinda nice to see Arlene on the defensive for a change. And Kimberly was off and running. "Your campaign funded free drinks at the soft drink machine yesterday, right?"

Arlene and Marcy sounded like the Dynamic Duo. "So?"

"What happened to all those cans? Were there

any bins to recycle? No!"

"That's not Arlene's fault!" Marcy jumped in.

"Who is responsible then?" Kimberly shot back. "If she wants to be president, how can she simply shift the blame on all the issues?"

Well, E.D., Arlene must have realized that she was losing the "issues battle," because she immediately went on the attack in the only area she really knows best: clothes.

"And what about Drea Thomas?" she said to the crowd. "She breezes into school on an old bike wearing a combination of clothes that *I* wouldn't wear for Halloween. Is that who you want representing you on the Student Council?"

Now, that comment about my clothes and Halloween made me mad. What's wrong with vests and baggy shirts and neckties and saddle shoes, anyway? This was an attack on the individual spirit!

"Yeah," Marcy chimed in. "Drea may be a great baby-sitter . . . but are we babies?"

Couldn't help it, E.D. "Well, I guess some of us *are*," I said.

I could see that the boys were getting a big kick out of this. "Hey, this is getting *good*," George said gleefully, poking Bobby.

I'm not sure what would have happened next, but we were literally "saved by the bell"—except that Mrs. Long also came by just then. "Okay, folks, let's all head for our next classes," she said. I was just about to make my escape when she put her hand on my shoulder. "Drea . . . I need to talk to you."

Uh-oh. Suddenly I had a real sinking feeling. I mean, what Kimberly and I had been saying all made sense in the heat of the moment, but I wondered how much Mrs. Long had heard and what *she* was going to say. Didn't take long to find out.

The principal was carrying one of Arlene's posters which she held up—one with a moustache drawn on Arlene's face.

"I'm really concerned about what's happening here," she said gravely. "The Drea Thomas that takes care of my kids three afternoons a week is a caring, creative, responsible, loving, fun person . . . but the Drea Thomas who is running for class president is none of that. She's spreading rumors, defacing posters, bending the truth . . . What's going on?"

I wanted to protest, to say that I hadn't drawn that stupid moustache . . . but the lump in my throat right then wouldn't let me even squeak.

But Mrs. Long went on anyway. "I think you need to decide for me . . . for yourself . . . and for the school: who is the real Drea Thomas?"

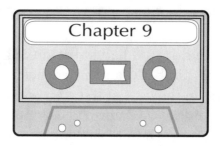

The Fish that Cried Shark

The real Drea Thomas? I don't know if I know anymore, E.D.! Here I am, sitting on our balcony, thinking back over everything that happened today . . . and I feel so confused. Yesterday I took on this campaign feeling kinda like Robin Hood squaring off with the scheming Sheriff of Nottingham—but now even Mrs. Long says she can't see any difference between the good guys and the bad guys!

All that stuff about animal testing and environmental policies was Kimberly's idea . . . still, it *is* my campaign, and I did buy into the idea that we gotta beat Arlene at her own game if we want to win the election. But . . . politics is politics, right? After all, we didn't really tell any lies . . . just maybe stretched the truth a little. At least our motives are good. After all, I *would* make a better president than Arlene . . . but . . . it seems like in order to win, ya gotta bend the rules of the game. Except . . . now the game's getting kinda muddy.

And that's not all that happened today, either.

When I got home from school . . . feeling about two inches high after Mrs. Long talked to me . . . Matt was in a real funk. Even Rebecca was worried about him. She pulled me aside and said that Matt had stepped ON the cracks in the sidewalk all the way to school this morning—and didn't even notice.

Actually, Matt looked like I felt, so we didn't talk much at first. He flopped on my floor pillows and buried his head in a book . . . Rebecca, conscientious as always, was doing her homework at my desk . . . while I stared at the maps on the slanted ceiling above my bed and wished I could transport myself via time machine to Timbuktu—at least until after the election.

After a while I decided I might as well clean up the art supplies Matt and Rebecca had been using to make campaign posters for me yesterday. I started to pick things up . . . when I saw some of the papers Matt had been painting on hidden under the pile of posterboard. I glanced at Matt and Rebecca . . . both were busy with their books . . . so I slid out the pages and turned them over.

It was Dad's missing music sheets—with streaks of red and blue paint glopped all over them.

Just then Rebecca jumped up and said, "Okay, I can't stand it anymore! Isn't someone going to talk? You guys are real downers!"

I quickly pushed the music sheets back and looked at Matt, hiding behind his picture book. Dad *had* laid his music sheets on the kitchen table, and they'd gotten mixed up with the art supplies . . . and Matt knew it. No wonder he was in a funk! But I was beginning to get an idea . . . an idea for a Secret Adventure.

I pounced on Matt and the pillows. "Rebecca's right. We all need an adventure!" I motioned her to come down on the floor with us.

Matt shook his head vigorously. "No way!" he protested. "I'm not in the mood for one of your crazy adventures. I'm too busy reading this . . . uh . . . fish book."

A fish book . . . a fishy story . . . ah-ha! That was it.

"Come on, come on," I teased him. "You don't need to stop reading your book. We'll just come along with *you*. Here we go-o-o!" . . .

I grabbed Matt and Rebecca and we all clung tightly together as my attic room began to swirl around and around, faster and faster, until it seemed to spin right off the rest of the house.

"Oh, noooooooooooooooo . . ." Matt cried, hanging onto his fish book.

Wood floor, rag rug, and floor pillows disappeared . . . and in their place appeared a "floor" of white sand with sea sponges, waving seaweed, and slimy, brown kelp sprouting every-where. A long lost treasure chest sat rusted and forgotten in the clear blue waters of a tropical sea.

"Whoaaaa!" yelled Matt. "I'm . . . I'm underwater, but I'm not drowning!"

"Yooowww!" yelped Rebecca. "Me, too!" Then she looked at Matt and began to giggle. "Whoever heard of a puffer fish wearing a baseball cap?"

Matt's eyes were as big as sand dollars as he twisted and turned, trying to look at his stubby fish shape.

"You should talk," he gurgled. "I

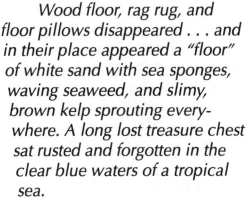

85

never saw an angel fish with glasses before, either."

Rebecca preened her long, flowing fins that arched above and below her with their black stripes—and peered around the ocean floor through her wire rims. "But . . . where's Drea?" she wondered.

"Here I am, guys," I said . . . swimming in a graceful circle around the two little fish.

"Wow!" said Matt. "Drea's a dolphin! I love dolphins!"

"But I never saw a dolphin wearing a vest and blue tie before," Rebecca pointed out.

Oh, well, she's new to my Secret Adventures . . . I knew she'd get the hang of it soon.

"Look at us! This is cool!" Matt said, testing out his fins. When he wiggled them one way, he went forward; another way, he went backward. "Hey . . . I can even go sideways!"

As for me, I'd always loved to watch the dolphins do their tricks at the zoo, so I tried a few underwater stunts myself.

"What in seaworld are you doing, Drea?" asked the angel fish in Rebecca's prim voice. "Why are you getting all twisted up like that?"

I untangled my tail from my snout and

grinned sheepishly. "The dolphins at the zoo make those tricks look so easy," I confessed. "Guess it takes practice."

But I knew something that DIDN'T take practice. "Tag! You're it, Matt!" I said, poking him gently with my snout and then darting away.

The puffer fish took off after Rebecca and me, as all three of us swooped and zig-zagged, playing tag among the waving strands of kelp and exploring the big rocks dotting the ocean floor. It was so much fun shooting to the surface and diving down again into the warm tropical water . . . without having to take swimming lessons!

But right in the middle of our game, Matt suddenly back-paddled his fins and said, "What's that noise?"

"What noise?" said Rebecca, the angel fish, looking around the sea floor.

"Hmmm," I said, listening. Then I heard something, too. "Sounds kinda like an underwater stampede."

Just then a school of terrified minnows darted across the ocean floor, pushing and shoving each other out of the way as each one tried to get ahead of the others.

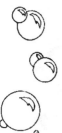

"Get outta my way" . . . "Me, first!"
. . . "Move over, fin face" . . . "Hey,
watch it, shark-bait!" . . . "Quit hog-
ging the fast lane" . . . "Run silent, run
deep, pal" . . .

"Hey, what's up, guys?" I asked the
little fellows. But the minnows ignored
me. I might be big, but I guess no one's
afraid of a gentle dolphin. Besides,
they seemed in too much of a hurry to
stop and chat.

But just then we heard another
sound—this one loud and urgent.

"SHARRRRRKK! Swim for your life!
Sharrrrrrrkk!"

The angel fish's eyes grew even
rounder behind Rebecca's glasses.

"Shark? Oh, no! What are we going to
do, Drea?"

Suddenly I felt a little anxious. What
had I gotten us into? I urged Matt and
Rebecca to swim quickly toward a
small cave entrance under one of the
rocky shelves. But Matt was scared . . .
and was beginning to puff up like a
round balloon.

"Oh, guys . . . help!" he cried, as he
started to float away from us.

"Matt, come back!" called the angel

fish. "What are you doing?"

"I can't help it!" yelled Matt as he continued to puff larger and larger.

"Oh, no!" I said, remembering what I'd read in the fish book. "When puffer fish get scared, they inflate."

"Inflate? Drea, do something! He's getting away from us!" yelled Rebecca, as she watched Matt puff up and float out of reach.

Just then an orange and white and purple striped clown fish tumbled into view in a cloud of bubbles. "Ah-haaa-ha-ha-haaaa!" he guffawed loudly. "What a bunch of suckers you floaters are. You really fell for that one . . . 'Oh, sharrrrrrrkk!' . . . haaa-ha-ha-haaaa!"

The puffed up puffer fish slowed to a stop. "You (burble) mean . . . no shark?" Matt said, barely able to sputter out the words.

"I guess not," I said, disgusted. The clown fish obviously thought he was very funny.

With the danger gone, the puffer fish relaxed just a tad too quickly—and shot around the ocean floor like a blown up balloon that'd just been released. Whooooo-ooosh!

"Whoa, there," said the clown fish as Matt shot by. "What do we have here? New fins in town?"

Rebecca swam right up to the clown fish and looked him in the eye. "So, there isn't a shark?"

"Oh, oh, oh!" laughed the clown fish glee-fully. "Little Miss Angel Fish sees right through me! . . . Of course there isn't a shark. You think a smart clown fish like me would be floating around if Jaws was on the loose?"

Matt was finally back to his normal shape and swam over to the clown fish. "You lied to us!" he accused.

"Lied?" said the clown fish, looking shocked. "No, au contraire, little buddy. Just a little prac-tical joke . . . aqua humor . . . fish frivolity . . . Hey. I gotta flip, dudes. It's been real. And here's a little advice. Get a sense of humor, Puffy. Haaa-ha-ha." With that, the clown fish swam away, chuckling to himself, leaving the three adventurers alone again.

"Puffy??!!" said Matt, looking offended.

"Don't worry about it, Matt," I told him. "Come on, let's forget about that joker and explore some more."

The ocean floor was a maze of exotic plants, sea shells, an old rusted anchor, and scurrying crabs. It was fun gliding in and out of the sea-weed with just the flip of a fin. Pretty soon we forgot all about the clown fish . . . especially when we swam over a little sand dune, and there, nestled in a dip in the sandy bottom we saw the most amazing sight: the broken frame of an ancient sunken ship resting on its side.

"Wow!" said Matt. "Maybe it was a PIRATE ship!"

"Who knows?" I said, poking my long dolphin snout into a porthole.

I was just about to wiggle inside when I heard the angel fish call me. "Wait, Drea!" gulped Rebecca. "What was that shadow?"

"What shadow?" I asked.

"Up there . . . on the surface."

I backed out of the ship until I could get a good look upward. And sure enough: a long, menacing gray shape floated high overhead . . . back and forth . . . back and forth.

"Drea!" said Rebecca, her long fins trembling. "This time it really is a shark, right?"

It certainly looked like a giant thresher shark silhouetted against the surface. But you can bet a can of tuna I wasn't going to wait around to find out for sure. "Come on!" I cried to Rebecca and Matt. "Let's get out of here!"

But without realizing it, we had drifted away from the seaweed and rocky caves and even the the old sunken ship. I looked this way and that . . . but only sand stretched in all directions. There was no place to hide! I began to swim frantically in circles, with Matt and Rebecca right on my tail, looking for cover. But the shadow overhead followed us, and it was coming closer and closer.

Frightened, Matt began to puff up again . . . and started to float toward the surface, right toward that awful gray shape. "Help! Help! I'm puffing again!" Matt cried.

Rebecca darted at him again and again, trying to bump Matt back toward the sandy bottom, but in spite of her valiant efforts, the angel fish was too small to keep the puffed up puffer from floating up . . . up . . . up.

The situation was getting serious! I had to do something! With a strong thrust of my tail and flippers, I quickly swam upward, placing my long dolphin body as a shield between the two smaller fish and the enemy overhead.

"Watch out!" screamed Rebecca. "Here it comes!"

The shadow loomed closer and closer. This was it! We were a shark snack now! I couldn't bear to look . . . but as if on cue, all three of us let out a terrified scream:

"Aaaaaaaaaaaahhhhhhhhhhh!"

There was a deathly silence. And then . . . a familiar laugh.

"Haaaa-ha-ha-haaaa-ha! GOTCHA!"

Slowly opening our eyes, we looked up . . .

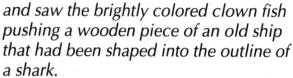

and saw the brightly colored clown fish pushing a wooden piece of an old ship that had been shaped into the outline of a shark.

"Heh-heh-heh . . . works every time with the tourists," the clown fish chortled. "Scared you guys, huh?"

Matt and Rebecca and I were almost speechless with anger.

"You—you—you're mean," Matt spit out, gradually beginning to de-puff in a swirl of little bubbles.

Rebecca wasn't looking very angelic for an angel fish. "What if there was a REAL shark. What then, Mister Clown Fish?" she demanded.

"Oh, oh, oh," chuckled the clown fish, "Little Miss Angel Fish is SO worried. Listen, sister, sharks are just big dumb slabs of blubber with teeth. Anyone who gets eaten by a shark deserves it."

With that, the clown fish did a little two-step on his tail fins. "Well, ta-ta. Time to blow. Don't eat any wooden minnows . . . heh, heh." And he swam off merrily.

I watched him go, shaking my head. "That is one mixed up fish," I said. "Doesn't know a lie from the truth—and it's gonna get him in big trouble one of these days."

I had hardly gotten the words out of my mouth when a large shadow passed over the ocean floor. Quickly, I looked up, expecting to see the clown fish pushing his makeshift wooden shark around again. But there was something different about this large, gray shape . . . its strong tail swished back and forth, thrusting its huge body in threatening spurts through the warm, tropical waters. And then I saw it: a large mouth full of sharp teeth, and a wicked gleam in its eyes. I was just about to dive for cover, when, with a tip of its fin, the thresher shark disappeared in the same direction the clown fish had gone.

"Sharrrrrrrrkkk!" Matt and Rebecca screamed together. I joined in. "Swim for your life! REAL sharrrrrrrrrkk!"

A mocking voice answered from beyond the next patch of seaweed. "Ha-ha, can't fool me. I'm the trickster, remember? Ya gotta do better than—whooooaaaahooohooo! Help! Help! Reaaaal sharrrrrkk!"

And in a burst of bubbles, the clown fish came darting past, finning its way frantically ahead of the huge thresher shark, who was snapping at its tail with those big, sharp teeth.

"Help! Help!" yelped the clown fish. "That 'big dumb blubber' thing was a joke . . . honestly! Help! Yeeeoooooooowwwwww!"

We watched in horrified fascination as the clown fish and his pursuer were soon lost in a maze of seaweed and waving kelp, churning the peaceful tropical waters in a swirl of bubbles, swirling . . . swirling . . .

Just then Dad's familiar voice boomed up the attic stairway, bringing our Secret Adventure to an abrupt end as we landed back on the floor of my room, all of us gripping the fish book.

"Matt! Rebecca!" he called. "Your mother's here! Time to go!"

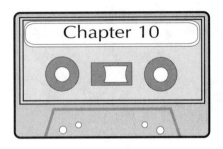

Chapter 10

Weed Whackers and Soccer Secrets

Hearing my dad's voice, Rebecca grabbed her schoolbooks and bolted out of my room like a streak of lightening. Guess our shark escapade was a little too nerve-racking. But Matt was still gripping the fish book he'd been looking at during our Secret Adventure.

"Drea?" he said thoughtfully. "What do you think happened to the clown fish? Did the shark eat him? Or did he get another chance?"

"I dunno, Matt," I said. "What do you think?"

He rolled off the floor pillows and got to his feet. "Well . . . I think maybe he should get another chance."

I watched as Matt went slowly over to the pile of

posterboard and pulled out the damaged music sheets. "Um . . . this is your dad's music," he said with a big sigh. "It got mixed up with some of my drawings when we were working on the kitchen table yesterday. I . . . um . . . painted on it by accident and . . . it's ruined." His face was so sad I thought he was about to cry. "I was too scared to tell you the truth," he said in a small voice.

He looked so brave standing there with the painted music in his hand that all I could do was give him a great, big hug.

"Your dad's gonna hate me," he mumbled sadly.

"Ahem . . . I doubt that very much," said Dad, who had come up the stairs just then and walked over to us. He took the music from Matt and looked at it.

It was definitely ruined.

But Dad just grinned his lopsided smile and said, "It was a mistake, Matt. I can live with that. We all make mistakes from time to time. The important thing is . . . you decided to tell the truth." And then Matt got another big hug, this time from my dad.

So. Matt 'fessed up to making a mess of my dad's music, and now he's got a big load off his shoulders and Dad's got his music back . . . well, at least he knows what happened to it.

Wish it was that easy to untangle the mess I'm in. I was glad when everyone left, 'cause I really need some time to think, E.D. It's so peaceful out here on the balcony . . . leaves beginning to turn color on the trees . . . evening sun turning everything gold and blue . . . but I sure don't feel peaceful inside. Ever since Kimberly shanghaied me into this election thing—

Oh! Hi, Grandpa! I didn't hear you . . . no, it's okay. I'm just thinking out loud to my electronic diary here. . . . Sure, come on out on the balcony. Just don't trip over that doorsill.

— *Click!* —

That was Grandpa Ben, E.D. Said he came over to return some of my dad's tools . . . but he sure does have an uncanny nose for sniffing out what people are thinking or feeling.

He could tell I was feelin' down, so I kinda unloaded on him . . . told him what happened today at lunchtime and what Mrs. Long said to me . . . it's pretty embarrassing. Seems like everything I've been doing for this election is for the wrong reason. I wanted to put a unique "spin" on my campaign— y'know, like George suggested—but everything seems to be "spinning" out of control, instead.

In fact, after taking Rebecca and Matt on that "fish-capade," I've been thinkin' . . . I'm a lot like that clown fish—bending the truth for my own purposes, not really caring who's getting hurt 'cause I think I have a good reason . . .

In fact, I told Grandpa, "I'm supposedly running to be an honest president—but I've become as rotten as the person I'm running against!"

Grandpa just leaned back against the house and watched the kids skateboarding along the street in front of our house . . . we've got a good view of the whole street from up here. Then he said, "Drea, what do we do when we find weeds in our garden?"

"Why, we pull them out," I told him.

Grandpa nodded. "Being a good gardener means you've gotta keep pulling out your weeds . . . 'cause if you don't pull the weed when it's tiny, it'll keep growing and spread through the whole garden and wreck it."

That's all he said. Then he gave me a hug, got up, and went back inside the house.

I *think* I see his point, E.D. But . . . I'm not sure I know how to dig myself out of the weed patch at this point! I mean, if I back out of the election now, Arlene will win, and I'm not sure I could stand her looking down her nose at me all year . . . but if I win, I'm not sure I'll be able to stand myself.

— *Click!* —

'Morning, E.D. Here we are in the Thomas kitchen . . . oh-seven-hundred and thirty hours. . . . Day 4,853 in the Secret Adventures of Drea Thomas . . . and I still don't know what to do. I'm supposed to prepare a final speech to give in assembly just before everybody votes . . . but so far, all I've got written down is, "Mrs. Long, fellow students . . ." period.

Glad I've got the kitchen to myself. Mom's gone to work already . . . and I hear Dad blasting away in the dining room on his "Sonata for Sousaphone." He must have rewritten the second movement.

Glad *he's* happy. The way I feel, I might as well be dressed in sackcloth and ashes, like the biblical prophets did when they were predicting doom and gloom . . .

I was just about to fix myself a piece of toast when my friend Mr. Toaster reacted to my remark about doom and gloom.

"Sackcloth and ashes? Ye-ouch! Kinda itchy and dirty, don't you think, Drea? Frankly,"—Mister Toaster wiggled his two handles with relish—"I prefer the outfit you're wearing today. Polka dot headband . . . white shirt . . . yellow vest . . . navy tie . . . gray stretch pants . . .

Yessirree, tutti-frutti. Looks like it's 'Dress for Success' Drea Thomas, the next seventh grade president of Hampton Falls Junior High!"

Now normally I enjoy a little verbal duel with a certain mouthy applicance. But today he popped out of my imagination, even though I wasn't in the mood. I decided to ignore him and dropped my bread in the toaster.

"Hey! Take it easy!" Mr. Toaster protested. "Don't punch my handles down so hard! You want your toast over-easy or extreeeeeeeemly WELL DONE?"

I went nose to nose with the toaster. "If you don't keep quiet today, Mr. Toaster, I'll 'sack' you and shake all your 'ashes' out!"

Mister Toaster retreated, his wires crossed. "Well, aren't we touchy this morning? Hu-umph already."

There . . . I rescued my toast. But I better get going, E.D. If I stick around here to write my speech, a certain ancient talking toaster will think it's his duty to be my ghost writer. And if I don't think of what to say soon, I may just be crazy enough to write it down!

Here we go . . . last round of the campaign. In a few hours, either Arlene or I will be going down for the count . . .

— *Click!* —

Day 4,853 continuing, oh-nine-hundred and thirty hours. I came to school this morning, E.D., determined to make the most of the last few hours before the actual vote. No more rumors, no more attacks on Arlene . . . just stick to *my* campaign, *my* qualifications, promote the idea of the student lounge—that kind of thing.

But the moment I walked in the school door, I saw kids reading some kind of flier and whispering to each other. Then Bobby Wilson walked by, flier in hand, looked at me as if he was really disappointed and said, "Very low blow . . . very low, Drea."

I didn't have a clue what he was talking about, but I grabbed one of the fliers off the floor, and it said:

TRAITOR!
ARLENE BLAKE
GIVES GAME SECRETS
TO SOCCER TEAM
ARCH RIVALS!

I was so shocked, I practically had to pick my chin off the floor. I looked around . . . and sure enough, there was Kimberly down the hall, passing out fliers left and right and calling out, "Hot off the press! Traitor Arlene Blake causes soccer fiasco!"

When I caught up to her, I waved a flier in her

face and said, "Kimberly, we've got to stop this—it's a total lie."

"No, it's not," she said lightly—and then shrugged. "It's . . . a partial lie."

"*Kimberly!*" I said, ready to blow a gasket.

But Kimberly was cool and confident. "Tell you what, Drea. You worry about your acceptance speech; I'll worry about the campaign."

"No," I said. "That's not good enough. I want you to stop this—NOW."

She was pretty offended. "That sounds like an order."

At her words, suddenly I became more confident. *I* was the one running for class president. *I* was responsible for what happened in my campaign.

"It *is* an order," I said. "I want you to stop all of this or . . . I'll fire you."

She just laughed at me. "*Fire* me?! I dare you to fire your best friend."

And so I did, E.D. I looked her right in the eye and said, "You're fired." Then I grabbed all the remaining fliers still in her hand and walked away.

But . . . I might as well admit it, my momentary surge of confidence has seeped away. It's now second period study hall . . . I asked the study hall teacher if I could use an empty room to write my speech . . . so here I am, about as deep in nasty weeds as someone can get in three days, and no weed whacker in sight. I've probably lost the election . . . I've probably lost my best friend . . . and I've probably lost Mrs. Long's confidence in me . . . unless . . . unless . . .

— Click! —

Wish me luck, E.D.! I finally decided what I want to say in my speech. Oh . . . there's the bell. Time for the assembly. Gotta run . . .

— Click! —

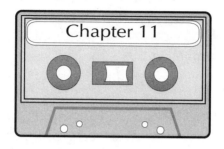

Voters and Victors

Unbelievable, E.D.! I'm back home in my room, and the last time I checked, I'm still in one piece. The election is over, the votes are in, and I'm still not sure what happened . . . but here goes anyway.

The election assembly finally rolled around, and I felt pretty queasy sitting up there on the stage with Arlene the Magnificent, looking out at the whole seventh grade class. The stage lights shone in my eyes, sorta like a bare bulb swinging slowly in a basement room while the cops waited for me to confess. I picked out a few faces . . . Marcy . . . Kimberly . . . George and Bobby . . . but it was hard to tell what each one was thinking. Mrs. Long introduced the candidates alphabetically and said we could each say a few "last words" before the vote— which meant Arlene spoke first.

I thought the auditorium was going to rupture when Arlene stepped up to the microphone! Marcy jumped up and led a cheering section who were chanting and stomping, "Ar-lene . . . Ar-lene . . . Ar-lene!"

Arlene was enjoying her moment of glory— okay, okay, I admit, I would've, too—but then she got on with her speech, which sorta went like this . . .

"Thank you, fellow students and teachers, for that rousing welcome." Then—I knew what was coming next—she held up the fliers Kimberly had been plastering all over school. "I suppose most of you have already seen this flier that my opponent has been distributing. This is symbolic of how she has run her whole campaign. Now, in my book, having dinner with my cousin, who happens to be on the Willowbridge Soccer Team, *doesn't* make me a traitor."

Ouch. That was the first time I'd heard where that rumor got started—and like Bobby said, the flier was a pretty "low blow." Then Arlene went on . . .

"That is simply a feeble attempt by someone who has no experience in student government, or as president of any organization, to try and discredit me."

She was right, E.D., but it sure wasn't easy eating humble pie in front of the whole class—especially since her whole tone of voice was so . . . so condescending. Anyway, then she said . . .

"I will guarantee that when I am elected, I will be the best, most qualified, seventh grade president Hampton Falls Junior High has ever seen."

At that point, Marcy and her cheering section went crazy, chanting, "Ar-lene . . . Ar-lene . . ." again and again. But when I got up to the podium, the cheers turned to an unmistakable hissssssssssss. A few people clapped, but by that time, I wasn't interested in prolonging the agony.

"I can't thank you for that welcome," I said, "but I do deserve it."

I thought for sure that Marcy's cheering section would let loose with a few hoots and catcalls, but for some reason the whole room suddenly got real quiet. So I went ahead with the speech I'd prepared . . . here—I'll read it for you, E.D. Excuse the frog in my throat. It isn't any easier reading it the second time around. Anyway, here goes . . .

"I was not prepared for what this campaign would do to me. I thought that I was running to represent the people of this school who didn't have a voice . . . but it became very clear to me that I was part of a campaign whose purpose was to ruin another candidate. I apologize to her, and to all of you, for that."

I turned to face Arlene when I made my apology, and she was looking at me as if I was a little green critter from Mars. I'm sure she didn't expect me to admit that she was right. But . . . I really did mean it. However, that wasn't all I needed to say.

"I also realized that what's most important about a campaign is honesty. I'm in Mrs. Roth's U.S. History class, and she's making us learn every known fact about George Washington . . ."

At that point, E.D., a lot of students laughed. Mrs. Roth is famous for her "pop quizzes" with "only" a hundred-eleven-thousand questions.

"But what stands out most to me," I went on, "is GW's complete and utter devotion to doing what was right and honest. Unfortunately, my campaign has betrayed the trust you placed in me. Therefore . . . I have decided to remove my name from the ballot."

That was all, E.D. I removed my "Vote for Drea" name tag, stuck it on the podium, and sat down. I could hear my footsteps echoing off the back wall of the auditorium . . . whoa, it was quiet.

I kinda held my breath, not sure what the reaction would be. Kimberly's mouth was hanging open, and I could tell she thought that I must have had a lobotomy. Arlene's face was twitching, as if she wasn't sure whether to look smug or suspicious. But both George and Bobby gave me a "thumbs up"—and that made me doubly sure I had done the right thing.

Mrs. Long's eyebrows had gone up in that okay-how-do-I-bunt-out-of-this-one look that adults get when an adolescent-type person throws them a curve. But, recovering nicely, she announced that even though Arlene was now the only official candidate, a vote still needed to be taken. So everyone's ballot was marked and collected and counted . . . and this is where it gets interesting, E.D.

Mrs. Long had a *very* odd look on her face when she got the final tally. She went to the podium again and said, "The votes have been counted. Arlene Blake has received 93 votes . . . "

Now, E.D., it only took a millisecond for 280 seventh graders to realize that 93 votes is *not* a majority. What was going on?

" . . . and George Washington—187 votes," Mrs. Long added.

I could hardly believe my ears! What in the world did it mean? My mind was spinning so fast, it took a second to realize that the whole auditorium was laughing. At first I thought they were laughing at *me* . . . but then I realized there were 187 write-in votes for honesty and integrity instead of popularity.

Mrs. Long held up her hand for quiet. "However," she went on, "considering that Mr. Washington spends all of his time at his monument, that makes Arlene Blake our new seventh grade president."

Of course, everbody in Mrs. Roth's U.S. history class knows that ol' GW isn't buried at the Washington Monument, but everyone dutifully clapped anyway. But for some reason, Arlene didn't seem too happy. It's true, she didn't exactly *win*, but she *does* get to be class president. Right?

As for Kimberly, she was absolutely ecstatic. "This is the coolest thing, Drea," she said, catching me as I came down off the hot seat. "You were honest and you *still* beat Arlene!" She was sparkling like a lit-up Christmas tree.

But then she did get more serious. "I'm sorry that I messed up you and GW. You probably could have won on your own. . . . Are we still friends?"

I was glad to hear her grovel a little bit—but I wasn't about to let her off the hook too easily. I mean, Kimberly meant well, and she's a very loyal friend . . . but frankly, she's the one who got me into this mess in the first place.

"I dunno," I said. "My dad would be pretty happy if I outgrew you . . . but . . . ." I shrugged and started to saunter off.

"Hey—wait a sec," Kimberly called after me. "I need a second chance. Maybe you could try out for the Cheerleading Squad!" . . .

I glared at Kimberly. If I didn't stop her now, she'd be managing my life for the next sixty years! (I can see it all now, E.D. . . . my whole life as managed by Kimberly Andow flashing before my eyes . . . Kimberly trying to negotiate a six-figure salary for cheerleading flunkie, Drea Thomas . . . Kimberly arranging blind dates for me all the way through college . . . senior citizen Kimberly volunteering her old friend, Drea Thomas, to lead the "March Across America" to save Social Security.)

But before I had a chance to get my hands on her, she flashed me that innocent Kimberly smile and sang out, "Just kidding!"

Just kidding, my foot. I may be able to forgive Kimberly for this election fiasco—but I'm not sure I'll ever let her pull me into another of her schemes!

Well, E.D., Mom wants me to help with dinner and I better see what Matt's up to. I've had all this time to catch up in my electronic diary because Rebecca was invited to go home with a friend after school, and Dad spirited Matt away as soon as he got here—for some "male bonding," he said mysteriously. Who knows what they're up to . . .

Wait a minute . . . What's that racket coming up the stairs? . . . Oh, no! It sounds suspiciously like . . .

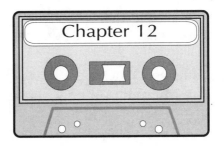

Terrible Tuba Tunes and the
Fantastic Food Fight

Wait . . . wait! Who said you guys could come in my room? . . . Oh, groan . . . Grandpa, don't tell me Dad's got you mixed up in this music medley, too . . . Where'd you learn to play the spoons? . . . Yes, Matt, I see you playing that—uh—kazoo . . .

Okay, okay, Dad, I'll listen to your Terrible Tuba Tune . . . Oh, *excuse me.* "Sonata for Sousaphone." Gotcha . . . I'll even record it on my electronic diary here . . . All right, blast away . . .

Oom-pah, oom-pah, oom-pah-pah-pah . . .
Clickity-click-click, clickety-click-click . . .
Bzzz-zzz-zzz, bzzz-zzz-zzz . . .

Oom-pah, clickity-click-click, bzzz-zzz . . .
Clickety-click, oom-pah-pah, clickety . . .
Bzzz-zzz-zzz, clickety-click, oom-pah . . .

. . . That's it? . . . Whew! . . . Bravo! bravo! . . .
Now, out, out! My room isn't big enough for tuba
concerts.

— Click! —

I just relistened to the impromptu concert Dad
and Matt and Grandpa had up here in my
room before supper . . . it's kinda hilarious, actually.
As I pushed them out the door, I saw they were
playing off the sheet music Matt painted on! Dad
just winked and said, "Matt's painting actually
helps the piece—so I've listed him as second com-
poser!" . . . which made Matt grin from ear to ear.

Both Mom and Mrs. Long arrived just as we got
downstairs, so *of course* the Terrible Tuba Trio had
to play for their new audience. I've never seen Mrs.
Long laugh so hard!

But frankly, E.D., Dad's been a great sport about
the music fiasco. I mean, he really does have the
Tuba Festival at the college next week. But to end
up having fun with the mess Matt made . . .

I just hope I can bounce back from the election
fiasco at school this week with my sense of humor
intact—if not my dignity . . .

Mom asked me to whip up some microwave

potatoes, but I suddenly got hungry for the real thing. So I actually *peeled* a bunch of Idahoes and while I waited for 'em to boil, I went out on the back porch where Grandpa was sitting on the steps watching the sky turn from flamingo pink to passionate purple.

"Pretty sunset," I said, joining him on the steps.

"Umm-hmmm," he agreed. Then he said, "I think you did a great thing today, Drea Thomas . . . that kind of honesty is very rare these days."

Coming from Grandpa, that was about the best compliment anybody could ever give me! If only he knew what a hard time I had swallowing my pride long enough to see what I needed to do.

"I think I'm beginning to understand why Great-grandfather preached on that verse from Proverbs so often," I said. "You know the one . . ."

"'Truth stands the test of time, lies are soon exposed,'" Grandpa finished for me—and then we laughed.

"Yeah, that's the one," I grinned. "Guess 'lies' includes half-truths and rumors and gossip, too."

"That's right," Grandpa chuckled. "Those nasty fellows are slippery—they come popping up into the light of day before ya even get your back turned. And it doesn't take long for most folks to see 'em for what they are."

I nodded. "But truth . . . the light of day just makes it clearer and stronger, right?"

"Right," Grandpa said—then gave me a big hug.

I heard Mom calling me to come mash the potatoes for dinner just then. So I left Grandpa on the porch to enjoy the last slivers of the sunset while I went back into the kitchen. The evening news was on the kitchen TV, and I stood watching it for a few minutes . . .

As I watched the TV cameras pan over the news set, the zoom lens pushed in close on the newscaster . . . hmmm, there was something familiar about that face . . . and suddenly, there was John Tesh again, looking straight into the camera . . . no, looking straight at me!  *"An interesting story coming out of Hampton Falls, New Jersey, this evening," he deadpanned, shuffling his papers. "In an unusual turn of events, it appears that George Washington was elected president of the seventh grade class . . . a stunning upset over a popular candidate."*

"Turn off that TV, will you, Drea?" Mom interrupted, oblivious to my sudden imaginary fame. "Here—if you're actually going to mash potatoes, use this to protect your clothes." And she tossed me Jamison's "Store of Stores!" promo apron.

I hate wearing aprons, E.D. They make me feel like a cross between "The Beverly Hillbillies" and Julia Childs. But I didn't want to hurt Mom's feelings, so I put it on, dumped the hot potatoes into the mixing bowl, and turned the mixer on high . . .

"Ye-oww!" yelped the toaster, as flying globs of white stuff splattered his shiny chrome . . . the counter . . . the wall . . . "Help! Help! Turn that thing off! Call the fire department! Call the National Guard! We have a kitchen emergency here!"

"Oh, sorry, Mr. Toaster," I said, with a helpless grin. "Just trying out a new 'spin' on the potatoes . . ."

"Very funny. Look at me," complained the toaster. "Hideous dabs and dribbles all over my smooth complexion. It's hard enough keeping up

117

looks at my age, without you . . . Hey! watch it,
Sis! How would you—ow!—like someone to
scrub your face wibh ah wathclophth . . .
splzzz."

Oops. Should've turned the mixer on low! I
quickly mopped up the blobs of mashed potatoes
that had sprayed around the kitchen, hoping Mom
hadn't noticed . . . but when I turned around she
was standing in the middle of the kitchen, holding a
platter of fried chicken and looking kinda surprised—with a glob of mashed potatoes right on
her nose.

"Uh . . . sorry, Mom," I gulped.

"Oh. No problem," she said airily. "I was just
thinking that that apron doesn't look half-bad with
mashed potatoes on it. A new look in realistic marketing. In fact," she said, setting down the platter
and grabbing the wire whisk from the gravy,
"mashed potatoes *and* gravy might be just the
thing . . ."

And would you believe it, E.D.? My *mother*—
Lauri Thomas, professional woman—started chas-
ing me around the kitchen, shaking that wire whisk
and splattering gravy on me!

"Food fight! Food fight!" yelled the toaster.
"What is this family coming to, anyway!
Humph! When I was a brand-new wedding

present forty years ago, did your grandparents act like this? Nooo-o . . . Ye-oww! Gravy in my slots! . . . Hmmm. Oh, well, if ya can't beat 'em, ya might as well join 'em. . . . Take THAT, Drea Thomas!"
And Mr. Toaster let fly with a spray of burnt crumbs that had collected at the bottom of his slots.

Well, E.D., I vaguely remember Grandpa peering in the back door and Dad standing in the kitchen doorway—both of 'em staring at Mom and me as if we'd lost all our marbles. Somehow we got supper on the table—with *most* of the mashed potatoes and gravy—but every time somebody started to say something serious, either Mom or I started giggling hysterically all over again.

Guess Dad decided we all needed to let off steam after this "Week of Weeks," so he announced he was taking us all *bowling* after supper—even Grandpa. I thought bowling was only for people who like to wear matching purple shirts that say Bud's Drive-In or A-Z Hardware on the back . . . but Dad politely informed me it was a great game, and we ought to reclaim it for families, since anyone can play from seven to seventy. And he was right! It was a lot of fun . . . of course, my score was only 43 compared to Grandpa's 120 . . . man, was he smug. But I decided I have a pretty great family, even if they are a little crazy—present company an exception, of course.

I mean, who, me? crazy?

Don't bother to comment, E.D. *Your* job is to listen . . . though if you have any bright ideas about why I agreed to help Grandpa pull weeds from the garden tomorrow, let me know. He said something like, "As long as you're pulling out the weeds in your life, Drea . . ." and the next thing I knew, E.D., I'd signed up for D.D.—that's short for Dirt Duty.

Oh, well. It's the end of Day 4,853—a verrry long day in the Secret Adventures of Drea Thomas. I'm so tired, I feel like I could sleep for a week . . .

And that's the truth.

— *Click!* —